HUMANS

ARE WEIRD

I HAVE THE

DATA

BETTY ADAMS

Author Betty Adams

«Book Formatting by Derek Murphy @Creativindie»

Humans are Weird: I Have the Data

Copyright © 2021 by Betty Adams

Edited by Richard Wong

Cover Copyright © 2021 by Betty Adams & Adelia Gibadullina

For information contact :

(bettyadams@authorbettyadams.com)

http://www.authorbettyadams.com

Book and Cover design by Betty Adams

Cover art by Adelia Gibadullina

ISBN: 9781736003947

First Edition: November 2020

Second Edition: January 2021

Third Edition: March 2021

Fourth Edition : March 2023

3 2 1 10 9 8 7 6 5 4

Humans Are Weird – I Said I Liked It

"Greetings and salutations, Friend Dodge!" Quilx'tch called out as six of his legs scampered over the main countertop of the cafeteria.

Survey Core Ranger Mack Dodge turned to look at him, and Quilx'tch clutched his tablet to his abdomen tightly. He was no expert in human physiology, but Friend Dodge did not look good. The skin under his twin eyes was sagging in a way that would indicate the terminal stage of a rather horrific infection in one of Quilx'tch's people. The broad span of Friend Dodge's shoulders slumped several degrees down from the usual square he held them in. This made climbing his back to perch on them rather awkward. Quilx'tch did not know the proper protocol for asking humans to square their shoulders. Furthermore, Friend Dodge's mouth was twisted into that odd expression – humans' creepily flexible mandible coverings were so hard to read – was it a grimace?

"Friend Dodge!" Quilx'tch called out in shock. "Are you capable of keeping your eyes open?" Even a new-molted fellow like Quilx'tch knew that humans needed to keep the fleshy coverings on their eyes closed for a good portion of their rest cycles. At the moment, Friend Dodge's were barely half-open and twitching spasmodically.

"Hey, Quick," Friend Dodge slurred out, his cavernous mouth opening in a great gasp to draw in air. "Mostly, I guess."

Quilx'tch tried to make sense of this as he approached the human and kept pace with him. "Are you ill, Friend Dodge?" Quilx'tch asked as they reached the section of the cafeteria bar dedicated to the human's heated drinks.

"Ill?" Friend Dodge replied. "Nah, just up too late last night. Didn't get to bed till oh-dark-thirty."

1

Quilx'tch paused and tapped his hindmost leg thoughtfully against the counter top. "I am not familiar with that temporal designation, Friend Dodge," he finally confessed.

"Eh." The noise Friend Dodge made was indistinct and not followed by any clarification, so Quilx'tch watched patiently as the human chose his drink elements and prepared them.

"Interesting," Quilx'tch commented as Friend Dodge began sipping out of the cup of steaming water with a happy sigh. "The symptoms of sleep deprivation are fading."

"Good old yellow bag tea," Friend Dodge explained, holding out the cup. "My favorite poison."

"I have heard that statement before," Quilx'tch observed. "However, forgive me, but I must doubt that what you are consuming is actually poison."

"It's a figure of speech," Friend Dodge said with a chuckle. "Just means that the item in question is my preferred stimulant," he paused and tilted his head to the side. "But it is used for depressants too."

"I see," Quilx'tch said, rapidly taking notes on his tablet.

"Oh, good heavens, how do you drink that swill?" a third voice cut into the conversation as another human approached.

Quilx'tch glanced up in surprise as the second human brushed past on his way to the food counter, not stopping for an answer to his question. Friend Dodge only grunted at the other human and resumed drinking his tea.

"He does not share your opinion of the quality of this beverage," Quilx'tch observed.

"Sure he does," Friend Mack said with a grin. "The stuff is swill."

"But you just said it was the best," Quilx'tch protested in

confusion.

"Nope," Friend Dodge said, shaking his head. "I said that I liked it, not that it was good. There's a difference there."

Quilx'tch stared blankly at Friend Dodge, hoping that the human would at least try to explain that bit of nonsense, but Friend Dodge only finished his tea and left with a cheery wave. Quilx'tch watched him go and slowly entered his observations into his tablet.

Odd. Odd indeed.

Humans Are Weird – Persistence

"Are you sure you don't require aid?" Quilx'tch asked uneasily.

The nutritional anthropologist was clinging to the underside of the damaged cargo transport easily enough. The steel bar that supported his six motile legs was more than strong enough to hold his slight weight. No, the unease came from flecks of iron-rich blood that he could smell scattered on the underside of the frame.

"I have this, Quick," the human mechanic snapped.

Quilx'tch fell silent but didn't leave. The human was writhing around in a most disconcerting way. Granted, the odd movements of human joints were usually a little disturbing to any species with a proper exoskeleton, but Quilx'tch was fairly certain that human arms were not supposed to bend like that. The pain-filled grunts the human was letting out confirmed his suspicions.

"I know I could not be of use in a task that requires such raw strength," Quilx'tch began uneasily. "It would really be no trouble for me to fetch another human to aid you."

"I can do this myself!" the human growled. "I don't need any help."

Quilx'tch wondered at the hostility in the normally friendly human's voice. What possible benefit could the human gain by insisting on performing a noncritical maintenance operation that clearly was meant to be done in pairs? Especially as there were many other humans close to aid him? A loud snap coincided with a triumphant crow from the human.

"See!" the human called out. "I told you I could do it myself."

"You did," Quilx'tch replied. "Though I do not know why you make a point of that as I never expressed doubt that you could."

The human stared at him blankly for a moment and then burst into laughter. He rolled out from under the transport and sprang to his feet. Quilx'tch followed him and climbed up on the proffered hand. The skin on the hand was torn in several places though the human's remarkable healing factor had already stopped the bleeding.

"Yeah, I got a stubborn streak, I guess," the human said, shrugging his shoulders as Quilx'tch climbed up his arm. "Sorry I snapped at you."

"Apology accepted," Quilx'tch replied. He wanted to pursue the matter, but the human stretched and bent to pick up his tools.

"Come on, let's get lunch," the human said. "I get even more bull-headed when I'm hungry."

Humans Are Weird – Warm Spot

The main community hall at Rough End Base was never really clean or orderly. The attempt to provide furniture fit to the needs of roughly a dozen species had been successful from a practical point of view. The various relaxing devices that surrounded the one long couch provided texture and density comforting to the respective bodies that they had been designed for, but a general ignorance of color theory and the cluttered appearance made the space look more like a disordered maintenance hangar than a lounge of any sort. Though the various lounging humans and Undulates didn't seem to mind as they read, ate, or napped.

The breadbox-sized aliens that looked more or less like a cross between a wet mop and a loaf of bread were perhaps the main frequenters of the community hall. They were a very social species and enjoyed interspecies interactions even more than humans. They also found the frigid, arid nature of the desert base fatal for extended periods, making evening strolls inadvisable. So it was no surprise to Dr. Sharon when three of them approached him with their gripping appendages raised in greeting. He set his book aside and smiled widely at them, showing his less than perfect teeth.

"Hey there, my moppy friends, what gives?" he greeted them. He had long ago given up on identifying individuals among the earth-toned Undulates, and thankfully they didn't seem to mind.

"Greetings, Dr. Sharon," the one at the front of the three said, its soft, mouthless voice seeming to come from the center of the mass of drooping appendages. "There was a strange sound outside the rear safety exit."

Dr. Sharon nodded and closed his book. "And you wanted the big bad human to go take a looksee," he said. "Sure thing, probably a rock-rat. I'll go chase it off."

He got up off the couch and ambled across the large room. He passed the storage lockers that lined the walls and ducked under the low (for a human) emergency exit at the rear. Even in the airlock chamber it was chilly, and Sharon shuddered as he stepped out the final door into the bitter desert night. He glanced around but didn't see any fist-sized arthropods. He shrugged and went back inside.

"They must have run off," Dr. Sharon called out as he came back to his seat on the couch. "I didn't see any—" he stopped talking and narrowed his eyes.

He glanced around the community room. It looked like every Undulate in the place was now grouped on the couch, their appendages pulled tight and pressing against one another. The mass was grouped where he had been sitting. Some clung to the back of the couch. Some were sitting primly on the seat. Some of these were tucked against the armrest. Some clung to where his legs had rested. In fact, they almost formed a near perfect map of where his body heat would have warmed the cushions.

"You heard a noise outside…" he said.

"That we did," one of the Undulates said cheerfully. A gripping appendage raised out of the mass and gestured to the spot beside them. "Thank you for reassuring us. Please sit back down."

"Sure," Dr. Sharon snorted and shook his head. He eased back down onto the couch, and the mass of Undulates seemed to flex and expand to press against his side from his ankles to his shoulder. A contented, sigh-like sound came from the earth tone mass. His book was produced by an appendage, and he accepted it with a wry grin. "Must have been a quick rock-rat," he said.

Humans are Weird – Regulations

Alliance Coalition Safety and Health Regulation 574.328 Subfile 749 Topic-Interspecies Interactions in Formal Settings

If a human crew member requests any volume/weight/length of substance that is in any reasonable measure explosive/flammable/reactive under the standard range of pressure, reflectivity, and temperature found on Alliance ships, you are to determine exactly what they intend to do with it before providing it. The human must provide exact details of their intentions for every measurement, or it will not be provided to them.

Addendum 1: "I have a really cool idea" is not sufficient explanation.

Addendum 2: The presence of moderately hazardous vermin is never sufficient explanation, and should the human in question attempt to use it as such, they should be immediately reported to the commanding officer.

Alteration 1: *under conditions no less that two standard deviations away from the standard range of pressure, reflectivity, and temperature found on Alliance ships and on worlds frequented by Alliance away teams.

Alteration 2: *under conditions where a human can survive for more than five minutes with a standard survival gear set.

***

Addendum 145: It is to be assumed that if there is a human on your crew, there will be spontaneous explosions/ignitions/reactions. All ships hosting humans or likely to host humans or likely to pass near ships hosting humans will take appropriate precautions. Please see *Alliance Coalition Safety and Health Regulation 1453.245 Subfile 543*

Humans Are Weird – Forgetfulness

"Hey, Twitch, buddy," Private Jones called out from the next room, the salutation interrupted by a yawn.

"Yes, Friend Jones?" Quilx'tch responded without altering his posture. His secondary legs were tapping lightly across the bottom of his abdomen, triggering the keyboard that was projected there. He might have used the data-processing station in the center of the large communal room, but that would require running around the edge of the human-sized space. The pathways that the humans had built into the walls were very useful to be sure. However, Quilx'tch was tired after a long day of observing the base commander engaged in 'hunting' and had much data to process. He rather preferred to use his personal device and stay right here in the comfy hammock that had been made with his comfort in mind, thank you very much.

"Do you by chance remember what I came in here for?" Jones asked.

Quilx'tch paused in the composition of his observations and slowly turned to face the door that Jones had stepped through. He tried to parse the words. 'By chance' indicated that the human thought that the likelihood that the answer would be positive was low. Quilx'tch mulled hard over what the rest of the question could mean.

"Why do you think that I would know what your intentions were by leaving the room?" Quilx'tch asked.

"Eh," Jones said, "maybe I said something to you…"

"You did not," Quilx'tch said slowly. "But that is the room that houses the foodstuffs. Perhaps you were hungry and wished to procure food."

"It's always about food with you," the human said with some

amusement in his voice. "Oh! Right. Boot grease! Thanks, buddy."

Quilx'tch stared rather blankly at the door as Jones came back in clutching the canister of 'boot grease' and proceeded to get to the task of cleaning and waterproofing his foot coverings. Quilx'tch thought to ask why Jones had thanked him when his suggestion had been fruitless, but the question of how the human had forgotten his intention between the couch and the door seemed both more pressing and less polite. Finally Quilx'tch shrugged and turned back to his report, making a high priority note to pursue this further. Such a sensitive topic as flaws in mental function might need something more in the way of diplomacy than a mere nutritional anthropologist could offer.

Humans are Weird – Bleep

"But why do the speakers produce different sound profiles?" Twistunder asked as he examined the earbuds in his grappling appendages.

"For directionality," Mack Dodge answered without taking his eyes off the screen. "It's why most interfaces have two speakers."

"And what is directionality?" Twistunder asked, pressing the earbuds to his lateral core curiously.

Mack paused as he tried to figure out the question. "So I am watching the two-dimensional screen here," he gestured at the screen.

"Yes," Twistunder said.

"So the lion-deer comes onto the screen from the left," Mack played back the scene. "Here at two-minutes-five, but you can hear him coming for about thirty seconds before that, right?"

Twistunder set the earbuds aside and waved his grappling appendages in agreement.

"So the computer knows to play the sound of the lion-deer from the left earbud so you know where to look," Mack explained. "What direction it comes from. So that is directionality."

Twistunder curled all of his appendages underneath him and sat there in what most of the humans on base called his 'thinking loaf.' "So humans," he finally said, "can tell which direction a predator is coming from by sound?"

"Well, yeah," Mack said. "Can't you?"

"No," Twistunder said simply. "Why would we need to do that? We can see where it is coming from."

Mack leaned back and examined the perfect radial symmetry of Twistunder's form. "You do have three-sixty vision," Mack agreed. "But what happens after dark or when you are in murky water?"

"Remember that we see well into what you call the infrared spectrum," Twistunder reminded him. "True 'blackness' or even darkness is very rare for our photoreceptors."

"Huh," Mack said. "So you just don't get much directional information from sound."

"And you use sound to avoid predation. This does explain some… if you do not mind me saying so… odd behavior of yours," Twistunder said.

"Oh, really," Mack said, leaning back with a grin. "Like what?"

"You wish to know what behaviors we find odd?" Twistunder asked carefully, his appendages shifting out of his thinking loaf uneasily.

"Yup," Mack said with a grin. "Give it to me."

Twistunder gave a low humming noise. "You… swivel… when the pressure alert sounds."

"Yeah," Mack agreed. "It is an annoying beep."

"You have common names for specific wavelengths of sound dependent on duration and intensity," Twistunder pointed out.

"Beep, boop, bleep," Mack said with a grin.

"That!" Twistunder said, raising his grappling appendages eagerly. "You name sounds!"

"I guess we do," Mack said. "What of it? You name specific wave shapes."

"It is just strange," Twistunder said. "Just a little strange."

Humans are Weird – Hunting About

"Are you sure you are okay with this, Twistunder?" Mack asked as he hefted his pulse rifle over his shoulder.

His companion crawled out from under the stack of backpacks that had fallen around him and twisted his front appendages up in a rough approximation of a thumbs up. Mack smiled down at the alien and carefully began stacking up the backpacks again. In the dim light of the storage room, the dusky gray Undulate might easily be mistaken for a rather matted wet mop. Mack stacked the last of the packs and hoisted his full one onto one shoulder.

"Are you ready to go?" Mack asked.

"Very ready," Twistunder assured him. "May I help you situate your pack?"

"Probably not a good idea," Mack said with a grin. "I still need to put a few things in it and get the carrier for my rifle."

Twistunder hesitated, and his appendages tapped the floor in a fidgety manner.

"May I help you adjust your backpack?" Mack asked with a grin.

"Please!" Twistunder lifted up the backpack, and Mack carefully slipped the small backpack over three appendages on each side of the Undulate and then set it on Twistunder's dorsal ridge.

"That is quite acceptable," Twistunder said after fidgeting for a few moments. "Let's go!"

"Why are you doing this again?" Mack asked as they proceeded towards the bay where the last of his gear was waiting. "One of the other humans could go with me instead, and I know you guys don't like to take part in taking the life of higher animals."

"This is an essential part of your culture," Twistunder explained. "And while we do not need or choose to kill higher animals for food, we do end their lives for self-defense purposes as you do as well. So the concept of hunting is not entirely foreign to us. I wish to both learn human hunting methods and overcome my own disgust reaction to what appears to be a fairly logical endeavor for you."

"Good goals, I guess," Mack said as a thought struck him. "Say, you guys are basically furry and cute, graze on algae, have pretty similar social rules about excrement and illness, and even your issues on reproduction are about the same as ours from everything I've heard."

"That is a fairly approximate summation of those cultural factors," Twistunder agreed.

They reached the airlock where Mack had left his stuff, and the Ranger quickly sorted out his pack while he talked. "Well, none of that falls anywhere near the human disgust reaction," he observed. "In fact, I can't think of anything a human would find disgusting about one of you."

Twistunder hesitated. "Was that a compliment of sorts, Mack?"

"Not really," Mack said as he shouldered his gun and triggered the airlock. They walked out into the dim red sunlight of the savanna together, and he checked his compass. "I was just thinking that it was kind of odd."

"We have not shared all of our culture with you," Twistunder said. "For better or for worse."

Mack grunted and sighted in on a particularly red outcropping of dunga trees that likely hosted the herd that their survey had indicated was just about to reach maximum carrying capacity.

"Well, at the moment we have some protein to procure, and if I have any sort of luck, you will get to test that disgust reflex by sunset. Care to climb up?" Mack held down a hand, and the Undulate happily climbed up his arm to rest on his shoulder.

Now Mack was all for cultural exchange, mind, but he was going to have words with whoever had taught Twistunder the words to 'A Hunting We Will Go.' The person who had taught him the concept of singing in rounds would come next.

Humans are Weird – What is a Dog?

"Looks like it'll be another rough day out there tomorrow, Bub," Chriton observed as he sipped his coffee.

Black, strong, and cheap as it could be bought. It was probably grown in a trash heap behind some factory in Chicago. If Bub had any opinion on the quality of his master's drink, he kept it to himself. His shaggy, white head was pointed at the door of the small mountain cabin in seeming idle interest in the howling of the storm outside. Occasionally his ears twitched at some squawk of the radio that was quietly muttering to itself on one of the rough shelves in the crowded room. The fire in the little potbellied stove crackled and thumped, and Chriton, a man who wore the title average with comfortable grace, got up to add another log to it. He had to move around a box filled with blankets and a pile of assorted bottles, nipples, and powdered milk; all stocked in anticipation of the arrival of several hundred new lambs that the mountain was expecting any day now. The fire tended to, Chriton turned his attention to Bub, who was whining softly and pawing at the door.

Chriton arched his eyebrows and examined the shaggy, white mass curiously. The dog's head was tilted to the side with curiosity, and there was the faintest sign of stress in the movement of the bushy tail and the knitting of the comical brown 'eyebrows.' Chriton sighed and looked at the clock ticking away on the wall. Three A.M. and a snowstorm roaring. If Bub needed help, there would be no way for Chriton to provide it to him out there.

"But you don't usually need help, do you, Bub?" Chriton asked amicably, walking over to scratch behind Bub's perked ears.

Bub waved his tail eagerly and let his tongue loll out of his mouth. Chriton sighed. He had just checked the ewes this evening, and none were nearer to lambing than three days; hopefully after the storm passed. If it were a wolf or a bear or even a coyote, Bub would be snarling murder at the door.

"Well, here's to you just wanting to go sniff an odd fox, Bub," Chriton said as he set his shoulder to the rough hewn plank door.

It took a massive shove from a man who was neither small nor weak to even open the door against the force of the wind, but Bub was out into the storm in a leap with nothing but glee in every fiber of his body. Chriton mused over what forty-odd years had taught him about sheep, chance, biology, and the ways of dogs and life and sighed.

"Just in case," he told the clock as he moved to the piled supplies.

He turned up the radio and let it fill the cabin with the mournful tones of Johnny Cash while he cleaned out the low-sided wooden box and layered it with battered but clean wool blankets. He set a pot of water to boil on the stove and lined up three bottles and nipples in the bottle holder that leaned against one wall. If there was a lambing ewe out there, Bub would know what to do. If the lambs were strong, hale, and wanted, Bub would soothe the ewe and curl close to her side to help keep it warm. If it were weak, sickly, or rejected, Bub would bring them to Chriton. Best to be prepared in any case. If a lamb was stillborn, well, Bub wouldn't leave anything to tempt the coyotes into developing a taste for mutton lying around.

The radio fell silent for a moment in the middle of the Folsome Prison Blues, and Chriton glanced up in interest as the emergency alert flared:

Highway 47 is closed from milepost fifteen to milepost thirty-two through White Pass due to inclement weather. Alternate routes are available along Drift Creek Road and Green Butte Road. The announcer stated: *Snow chains are now required down to a thousand feet. A convoy carrying various diplomatic officials, comprising three black Chevy Escorts, has fallen out of contact, and residents are requested to report any sightings in the closed area.*

The message was repeated a few times, and Chriton finished his preparations. He sat back down in his chair as Cash started singing again. As if struck by a sudden thought, he got up and pulled his smart phone out of a box on a shelf. He turned on the map function, assured it that it was no matter that there was no signal, and traced his finger along the red stripe of the highway and then the thinner black line of Green Butte Road. There were perhaps ten miles between the nearest point on the road and the hanging valley that sheltered his cabin. Chriton shrugged and wrapped a blanket around his shoulders before turning down the lamp and settling into his chair.

He was woken by the sound of scratching at the door and groaned as he untangled himself from the blanket. If there was no lamb, Bub would have barked to be let in; so much for sleep tonight. He wrenched the door open and closed it firmly behind the dog. He followed Bub sleepily to the lamb bed and knelt down, holding out his hands for the wee one. He didn't even fully open his eyes until Bub gave a low, frustrated growl.

Chriton forced his eyes open and stared dumbly at Bub's mouth. "That," he said softly, "is no lamb."

He staggered to his feet and turned the light to full power before returning to where Bub had placed the... something... in the lamb bed.

"Well, it's something all right," Chriton said as he knelt by Bub, "something that is supposed to be alive."

Chriton held the lamp over the tangle of drooping mop-like limbs. He hung the lamp on the wall hook set there for that purpose and reached out to gently untangle the creature. Bub whined in concern but didn't try to interfere. The muscles were stiff but not rigid and terribly cold. A few minutes of sorting out the mass revealed that the creature was longer than it was wide, and there was a pair of limbs that was a bit longer on one end and a bit rougher than all the others as if from hard use. Around one of these, there was a bracelet or ring or something that was intricately carved. Chriton eased it off and examined it. *Ambassadors and Friends* was etched around the inside. His brow knitted, and he glanced sharply at the creature in the lamb bed.

"What the flying scrap did you bring me, Bub?" Chriton demanded. "Or who?" He reached down and dug his fingers down into the mass of appendages until he touched the core they all attached to and frowned. He could feel no warmth. "Is it alive, Bub?" Chriton asked.

Bub chuffed softly and nosed the creature. His tongue licked out and ran over the appendages.

"I'll take that as a yes," Chriton said.

He took the pot of water and mixed it with some ice-cold snow until it was just a little warmer than his hands. He eased the creature into the pot, making sure to leave the end with the longer appendages and the jewelry out to breathe.

"I rather hope you breathe," he commented as he gently massaged the alien. "A diplomatic convoy, eh?" A thought struck him, and he glanced up at the clock. It was almost seven. "How did you run twenty miles in this in two hours?" Chriton demanded of Bub.

Bub waved his tail and slipped under a blanket that hung on the wall and led to the cooler firewood storage. Chriton sighed and continued his ministrations. After an hour, the alien began to move weakly. Soon it was fighting to slip fully down into the water. Chriton kept the front end – at least he hoped it was the front end – out of the water until a disgruntled voice demanded, "Would you please let me hydrate properly, Friend Human?"

The voice was odd, hollow in a way, and Chriton dropped the alien in shock. It hummed happily and began circling the bottom of the pot in an undulating motion. Chriton watched it circle for a moment and then shrugged and returned to his chair. He was just dozing off when the hollow voice sounded again, stronger this time.

"Pardon my intrusion into your sleep cycle, Friend Human. But could I bother you to add more thermal potential to the miniature biome?"

Chriton blinked dumbly at the mass of appendages sticking out of the pot and ran the words over in his head a few times. He grunted and staggered up to add some more hot water from the kettle. The alien wriggled happily and scooted to the side as Chriton poured the hot water in.

"Thank you, Friend Human," the alien said before submerging again.

"Do I call you Ambassador?" Chriton asked.

The alien paused and poked its *head* out again. "Oh, yes, that will do nicely. May I ask you a question?"

"Sure, Ambassador," Chriton agreed.

"How did you rescue me from that terrifying creature?" the Ambassador asked, its voice becoming less hollow and stronger as it warmed up.

"What terrifying creature?" Chriton asked.

"The large, hairy one with all the teeth," the Ambassador said, waving his appendages in what Chriton guessed was supposed to be an explanatory manner.

"Bub?" Chriton asked.

On hearing his name, Bub stuck his head out of the flap and looked expectantly at Chriton.

The Ambassador gave a soft squawk and ducked back into the water. "Yes, that is the one that I mean," the Ambassador said, the voice sounding out from the pot's sides.

"I didn't rescue you from Bub," Chriton said. "Bub rescued you from the storm and brought you to me for help."

"I see," the Ambassador said. "Is he quite safe?"

"For you?" Chriton asked. "Sure, so long as you are my guest, he will protect you."

"I understand," the Ambassador said. "Then perhaps I should bid you good night, my host. I must refresh my energy stores. But if you are willing, I would like to ask some questions about my rescue tomorrow."

The Ambassador dropped back down into the water and out of sight in the pot. Chriton blinked at him and idly wondered if this would all be a dream by dawn. He shrugged and sat back down in his chair.

"You and me both," he muttered. "You and me both."

Humans Are Weird – Compliments

"Ranger Mack Dodge! Your venting system is quite fragrant today!"

Mack twisted around and peered through the gaps in the inner workings of the hover truck he was attempting to fix. "My what is what now?" Mack asked.

The Undulate mechanic, who hadn't yet chosen a verbal name, proceeded to writhe his way up through the engine compartment only to pause just in front of Mack's face. The alien was the dusty maroon color that most Undulates turned when they were out of the water for any length of time. It was hard to get a good look at him as he twisted his vertebrae-free body through the small gaps in the engine. Mack resisted the urge to pull back as the swarming mass of pseudo-pods stopped just short of his face. The Undulate reached out with one gripping appendage and held it in front of his mouth like a microphone.

"Your venting system," the Undulate gestured at his mouth, "is quite fragrant today." The Undulate gave the portion of himself facing Mack a wiggle that suggested approval or pleasure.

"Oh, ah, thank you," Mack said. "Your, ah, color is a lovely shade of maroon today."

"Thank you for the compliment, Ranger Mack Dodge," the Undulate said.
Mack blinked at him. "I guess I will get back to fixing this hover truck now," Mack said. Turning back to his work.

The Undulate wriggled out of the truck, and Mack focused on clearing out the biomatter impacted in its undercarriage.

***

"How did your conversation with Friend Mack go?" the commander asked the mechanic as he swam back into the base.

"Oh, quite well," the mechanic informed him. "You were correct. Ranger Mack Dodge is quite friendly. Hopefully I will soon be able to call him Friend," the young mechanic paused and wiggled happily. "And perhaps he will feel comfortable enough to engage in the 'petting' ritual with me."

"Perhaps," the commander agreed. "Remember that humans do not communicate quite so much through touch as we do, so you must give him time."

"I understand," the mechanic said. He twisted around as if to go further into the base but paused at the door. "Humans do give the oddest compliments though."

Humans are Weird – Boredom

"Master Linguist?"

The hesitant voice pulled the linguist's attention away from his work on the datapad beneath him and up to the young one who crouched at the door. The Master Linguist let his vision slide over the youth, taking in the tightly held legs and the thorax pressed tightly to the floor. The apprentice linguist was nervous, excited, and probably shocked.

"Please come and loosen," the Master Linguist urged him.

The apprentice came forward with jerky movements and made a brave show of attempting to relax. The Master Linguist tucked his datapad away and moved over to run a soothing leg over the top of the apprentice's thorax. When the young one had sufficiently calmed, he began to loosen and rose to a more comfortable stance.

"You taught me that some of the greatest cultural discoveries happen not when you find the words that match but the words that have no direct translation. The ones we have to write whole paragraphs to describe."

"Yes," the Master Linguist agreed. "And why is this?"

"'Strange words describe strange ideas,'" the apprentice quoted. "If they gave it a word, it is very important to them. If we did not, it is elementally alien to us."

"And you think you found one of these critical words," the Master Linguist urged him gently on.

The apprentice waved one foreleg in distracted agreement, and the Master Linguist stiffened a bit. If it was not the trepidation of bearing an astounding claim to a skeptical superior, what was causing his distress?

26

"The humans—" the apprentice began.

The Master twitched. Oh, of course, the humans.

"They have a word that means they are suffering because there are not enough threats in their immediate environment. The soldiers in the base… they say they are bored."

Humans Are Weird – Nike

"Nike."

The word was spoken in such a dull, lifeless tone that it shook the rather rotund officer out of his stupor that was half bureaucracy-induced and half the result of the storm that was cracking dangerously over his talons. Commander Three Clicks's winghook paused over the report he was writing out, and he twisted his head to look at the young officer huddled on the floor. He had known that the field team had returned. He was not so {deaf} as that despite a long ago battle having shorn two of his rebounders off the top of his head. It had left him horribly scarred and flightless, but the remaining eight worked just fine, thank you very much, and he could get a nice feel for the safehold from where he hung in his office.

"Is that how an officer greets his superiors nowadays?" Three Clicks demanded sharply. "Lieutenant?" He had to squint a bit as the younger officer's fur was mussed far beyond regulation; come to think of it, he might not be able to fly safely – if at all – and Three Clicks felt a stirring of unease even before the lieutenant reacted.

The dark red wings rose in a shrug, releasing a waft of a strange and slightly unpleasant smell. *Human.* Three Clicks realized belatedly.

"Maybe. I don't know. It's important, I think."

Commander Three Clicks felt his fur bristle, and he raised his wings in irritation, but something stopped him. It was partly the dull look of resignation in the lieutenant's black eyes, partly the complete lack of reaction, and partly the result of the commander's torpor fuzzy mind finally catching up with the clues that were filtering into him. He had not heard the troop carrier that had taken the flight out return, and yet they were back. The storm was breaking over both the valley their safehold was in and the mountain slopes that the flight had been sent out to explore. They had been warned that they might encounter humans there.

"Lieutenant Five Trills," Three Clicks began, dropping down to the floor and coming close to drop a wing over him. "Is your flight safely returned?"

The young officer looked up at him dully and flicked his ears in uncertainty. "Every Winged that left with me has returned alive," he said carefully. "Injuries are non-fatal and healing well."

"That is a very specific report," Three Clicks observed even as relief flooded through him, and he guided the younger officer over to where a small bottle of leaf water from the home world sat beneath his perch. He poured out a glass of the drink for Five Trills and watched as the officer drank it with almost frantic eagerness. "What happened?" Three Clicks asked gently.

"We lost the transport about five thousand glides from the safehold," Five Trills replied, accepting another serving of water. "We had landed it at the base of a cliff to examine the surface for possible temporary holds. Private Ten Clicks stayed with the transport."

Three Clicks flicked his ears forward in acknowledgment. That had been their mission.

"We had taken observation on about half the face when a rock was dislodged above us," the younger officer went on. "I ordered the flight to retreat from the cliff face and… and…" Five Trills shivered and wrapped his wings around himself. "It was a cascade failure."

"Like in a computer system?" Three Clicks asked, laying his ears back in confusion.

Five Trills flicked his ears in confirmation. "Each rock hit another and dislodged it, and before we knew what was happening, the rockslide had engulfed the transport. It was buried under a mass of rock and detritus with Ten Clicks inside."

Three Clicks rocked back on his talons and stared at the younger officer in horror.

"We landed over where we thought the transport was and tried to move some of the rocks but—" Five Trills held out his wings, and Three Clicks could see that the manipulating ends were torn and scabbed from the attempt at the impossible task. "Private Twenty-seven Trills suggested that as we couldn't contact the safehold, we try to make contact with the human camp that was supposed to be in the next valley over."

Three Clicks flicked his ears at that. Spying on their new neighbors had been one of the secondary missions of that flight.

"We made contact, and the human technician there was eager to aid us. He was able to dig out what was left of the transport by the time the sun set. It was badly compressed, but we could hear that Ten Clicks was somehow still alive in the cockpit. Then the human pulled out one of those tools they always carry, and he just tore the transport apart," Five Trills explained with a few demonstrative twisting movements of his manipulators. "Ten Clicks was injured, not fatally, but he wasn't flying anywhere. That was when we remembered that the storm was coming. The human saw our distress and said that he could take us back to his base camp. All he had to do was summon his transport early."

"One of those whirlwind blades?" Three Clicks asked eagerly.

Five Trills shrugged his wings absently. "I do not know. That was when we discovered that some native fauna had taken out the communications array at his camp. We knew that we would not be able to survive the storm without a hold, and the human had a hard copy visual representation map, so he decided to take us back here to the safehold."

"But you said he had no transport…" the commander interjected.

"He had a harness," Five Trills explained. "We held onto it, and he did that human movement. The one they call running."

31

Three Clicks stared blankly at the younger officer for several heartbeats. "You are saying," he said slowly, "that this human carried you and your entire flight—"

"He carried Ten Clicks in a sling around his neck," Five Trills interjected absently. "Ten Clicks couldn't hold onto the harness on his own."

"*Five thousand glides* in the past day?" Three Clicks pressed on.

"Actually it was just over five {hours}," Five Trills replied.

Three Clicks rocked back again and cast his mind about. "Thank you for the report, soldier, but you should be in the medical bay," he said firmly. Just holding onto a harness moving at those speeds for that long must have been exhausting. "I will need to speak to this human—"

"That might be difficult," Five Trills interjected again as he let himself be led out of the room.

"Has he left in the middle of a storm?" Three Clicks demanded.

"No..." Five Trills clarified. "When we arrived in the safehold, he was leaking blood out of his mouth and nose. He asked us... was everyone alive, and when I confirmed it, he did that thing humans do where they show all of their teeth. Then he said, 'Nike,' and collapsed on the ground. The medics are trying to figure out if he is still alive..." Five Trills looked dully up at Three Clicks. "I said I thought it was important."

"Where are you going with that flotation device?" Quilx'tch asked his friend as the human passed by carrying a currently un-inflated raft. Quilx'tch was quite proud of himself for being able to identify the device. After all, emergency safety equipment was not really in the traditional scope of a nutritional anthropologist. However, when one worked with humans, one learned to expand one's horizons.

"The satellites are finally working over this area, and from the looks of it there's some awesome whitewater just south of here on the Widow Maker," the human replied with a grin. Shifting the giant device easily on one shoulder. "Smitty and me are going to try it out."

Quilx'tch carefully flexed the legs on one side to tilt his head in the manner that let the human know he was considering his words. 'White' was the term the humans used for their inability to distinguish between the visible color spectrum when several wavelengths were present at one time; how this modified 'water' was uncertain.

"So why are you doing this?" Quilx'tch asked curiously.

"Cuz it's gonna be fun!" the human replied with a wide and eager grin. "Hey! You want to come? It should be safe enough."

Quilx'tch was sorely tempted to join in the recreation, but every hair on his exoskeleton decided to fully extend at that moment.

"Aww, that is so cute when you do that!" the human crooned in genuine admiration, and from the way his fingers were twitching, Quilx'tch guessed he was fighting the urge to pet the anthropologist with his free hand.

"I am afraid I must decline," Quilx'tch said. "I have to prepare for a presentation."

"Well, have fun with that, you geek," the human flung the friendly insult at him cheerfully, and Quilx'tch chattered happily at his retreating back.

He had worked long and hard to integrate himself into the humans' social structure, and that they felt comfortable enough around him to revert to their habitual behavior pleased him to no end. Normally he tried to participate in as much of their recreational activities as he could but...

'Safe enough' paired with 'fun' usually translated into "There is a greater than 80% chance that I can bring you back alive from this situation," usually followed by "Hey, you can regenerate limbs, right?"

For the moment, Quilx'tch was quite content to go look up 'whitewater' and 'flotation device' in the database for now.

Humans are Weird – High Five

"Are you very certain that you do not mind me lingering here?" Twistunder asked of his human companion.

"Nah," Corporal Bryant said absently. "You just hang in there until we get these last sensors in."

"Agreed," Twistunder replied. He shifted a few of his gripping appendages on the warm skin of the human's back and carefully shifted the protection of the shirts that protected them both so that it lay easier over them. The scientist was acutely aware of the fact that his seeking shelter here left a large swath of the human's soft abdomen with only the thin protection of the 'tee-shirt' and a thin band of 'waist' with not even that. Twistunder rubbed his main gripping appendages together in guilt as he felt the solidified precipitation – what mad scientist could have postulated such a thing? – continue to strike the shirt above him. It stung a bit even through the protection of the human's clothing, and Twistunder shuddered at the memory of those horrible moments of pain before his companion had rushed to his side and sheltered him with his own body.

"You okay, Twist?" Bryant asked.

"I am," Twistunder hesitated, decided against correcting the shortening of his name, "still relatively uninjured."

The human gave a bark of laughter as they reached the next set of coordinates, and he plunged the spike that held the sensor into the soil. Twistunder felt a thrill of something that wasn't quite fear as he felt the bipedal muscle structure surge under his appendages. What raw power the human was capable of! What phenomenal forces their bodies were capable of absorbing. Perhaps he shouldn't feel quite so guilty about leaving the human with that bit of unprotected flesh. It was clear that even the tall, energy-expensive bipedal form functioned to protect Bryant from the precipitation as the small spheres struck his helmet and shoulders, then bounced away from the unprotected area.

"Two more left," Bryant said, and Twistunder could have sworn that there was joy and anticipation in the human's voice.

"You are excited because we are near the end of our task and the safety of our base?" Twistunder asked.

There was a pause, presumably because the human was accelerating his velocity. What did they call that type of movement? Running?

"Yeah, I guess," Bryant finally confirmed.

They fell back into silence, and Twistunder focused on attempting to read the confusing mix of chemical signals the human was sending out. This was a rare opportunity to study the humans up close, and Twistunder planned to make use of it despite his still lingering terror. Off to the east, the sky flashed with light that reached his photoreceptors even under the protection of the shirts, and shortly after that a horrific rolling *roar* passed over them. Twistunder fought down an undignified squeak of fear. Shortly thereafter Bryant plunged the next to last probe into the ground and laughed. Twistunder was suddenly struck by the idea that Bryant himself was a part of the storm. The power, the careless violence, the rolling noise, all was reflected in the sky and the surging body beneath the Undulate's appendages.

"One more!" Bryant called out. "And this last stretch is the shortest one."

Bryant accelerated and thrust the last spike into the ground. Freed of that last weight that had been pulling at his arms, the human altered his direction, and they began to fly over the ground. Twistunder became aware of some rising sound, something like a rivulet of water falling into the shoal from a prominence but loud and terrifying. Twistunder twitched as he realized that somewhere behind them the sleet had increased and the storm front that carried it was approaching them. Before the Undulate could ponder that much, Bryant gathered his muscles under him and simply *leapt over* the protective barriers that surrounded the base.

"Oh, security will not be pleased," Twistunder gasped.

Bryant laughed and charged the front doors of the base. They opened for him, and they passed through. Bryant decelerated violently and stopped in the center of the entryway.

"Whoo!" Bryant let out a sound that the xeno-psychologists would no doubt be analyzing for cycles to come. Bryant began moving around lightly, probably to allow his muscles to cool down without damage from his exertion, and Twistunder shoved a significant portion of himself out of the neck of the shirt in order to observe what was going on. The base's other human occupant was approaching them with a first-aid kit.

"Did you finish the mission?" the other human asked.

"Oh, yeah!" Bryant crowed. "High five, mate!"

Twistunder held on in shock as the humans raised opposing arms and swung them together with the same force that Bryant had driven the probes into the ground. The hands connected with a jar of force that traveled throughout Bryant's body.

"You ready to get down, Twist?" Bryant asked.

"Quite ready," Twistunder said meekly.

The Undulate climbed down the human's legs and slipped away to his quarters. He mulled over the idea of formally comparing the human behavior to a sort of benevolent atmospheric storm, a mad, mad, benevolent atmospheric storm.

Humans Are Weird – The Hero

"So why don't more aliens come to Earth now that the space port is open?" Mack asked idly of his companion.

The four-foot-long lizard blinked lazily at him with one eye and gave a snort of amusement. "Well, one might speculate that all that propaganda you sent out actually worked," the lizard rasped dryly.

"Propaganda?" Mack asked, arching an eyebrow. "What propaganda?"

The lizard kicked him reproachfully and stretched out in the warm sand. "Do not try to be obtuse, Friend Mack. I have seen the entire set you keep in your files."

Mack gave an interrogative flick of his foot, and the lizard snorted.

"I have watched the tales of the 'Hale Hero on the Abominable World' many times. If only a fraction of the horrors he revealed were true, no sane being would willingly come here."

"You are here," Mack pointed out idly, meanwhile wracking his mind for which of his shows his friend was referring to.

"Well, I have never laid claim to much sanity," the lizard confessed. "And I figured as long as I stick close to you, I will be safe from the horrors the Hale One faced."

Mack squinted over at him as his mind finished his mental tally. "Hey, the only files of mine that you've accessed are the David Attenborough documentaries…"

The lizard made the great effort to nod. "A Hale Hero indeed," he said seriously. "The man must be quite mad of course to face such horrors so easily, but his sacrifices are appreciated by all who have been warned away."

"Uh huh…" Mack eyed his friend and then decided that a nap was preferable to pursuing the odd conversation any longer.

Memo To All Rough End Base Personnel

While the base management does encourage all manner of interspecies interactions and especially the sharing of scientific information, we ask that all personnel respect these rules.

■ Organic biomatter shed from your person must be either handled as a potential biohazard and stored or disposed of properly. (We are aware that humans shed their skin and hair 'all over the place' and can only ask that they attempt to exfoliate in the washrooms as much as is healthful.)

■ If one intends to gift a portion of your shed biomatter to another scientist for the sharing of biological information and expansion of the general database, please ensure that said biomatter is packaged and labeled appropriately.

■ Biological samples are under no circumstances to be left in the refrigeration unit labeled for edibles. There is a separate refrigeration unit for samples, and it is clearly labeled as such. Use it.

■ If a human does happen to find an entire shed exoskeleton on top of the ravioli, it is requested that they read any accompanying notes before reacting.

On another note, the source of the 'unholy shrieks' experienced by several base personnel earlier today was traced to a particular human who does not choose to explain the source of their discomfort. They were uninjured. And further inquiries should be sent to the base commander.

Humans are Weird – Ideas

"Paper!" Accountant Lee yelled.

The shout sent an immediate gust of panic through the flight of soldiers surrounding her, and they shot into the air. Dozens of dark red wings flapped frantically as they abandoned the comforting bio-warmth she radiated to warily circle their human ally. This flight had never had to learn to respect human instincts in what the giant bipeds called 'the hard way,' but they knew the legends. If Lee suddenly leapt out of the couch she had been reclining in and held out her hands in supplication, screaming for 'paper,' they got her what she wanted.

"What kind of paper do you need?" the flight head asked, fluttering up to her face. When Lee froze and stared at him blankly, he cursed and remembered to lower his voice into human hearing ranges. "What kind of paper do you need?" he tried again, tilting his head to the side to catch the slow words of the reply.

"Something," Lee muttered, seeming to dismiss the worried flight and turning to dig through the couch. "Anything I can write on. And a pen or something to write with."

The flight head immediately ordered the second wing to fetch the note pad Lee had left in the kitchen. They swept off, and by the time Lee had found a writing utensil tucked in the cushions of the couch – *why on the wind would she store it there?* – they had returned with it clutched between their gripping claws. The frantic chirping of the wing caught Lee's attention, and she held out her hand to receive the notebook. She peeled her lips back and showed all of her blunt, herbivorous teeth in what the xeno-psychologists kept assuring them was a sign of pleasure.

"Oh! There it is. Thanks, guys!"

The flight members began talking back and forth, trying to figure out what danger the human needed the notebook to counter. She seemed ignorant of their distress and dropped back to the couch to start writing. The flight head silenced them and chirped a request to land on Lee's shoulder. She waved her assent absently, and he landed carefully on the broad surface.

"What exactly did you need the notebook for?" he asked.

"Oh, I had a great idea, and I needed to write it down before I forgot it," Lee muttered without looking up from the writing surface.

"What would be the consequence of you forgetting this great idea?" he pressed.

Lee glance up at him blankly for a moment. "I wouldn't be able to write it down," she answered him.

"So there is no immediate physical danger?" he asked.

Lee snorted and shook her head in a negative gesture. "Nah, I just needed to get this idea down," she said as she continued to write furiously.

An audible sigh of relief blew through the wing, and they settled back down in the warm aura of the human. The wing head gritted his teeth and began to mentally prepare the report on this incident. He really couldn't wait for the next wing head to rotate in. Humans were... disturbing.

Humans are Weird – Rope Swing

"The humans found the rope," Quartermaster Ctx'qlt said without preamble as he entered the conference room.

Quilx'tch clicked absently in sympathy without lifting his focus from the information he was presenting to the new commander. The commander however lifted his primary eyes to focus on the quartermaster. The commander's primary manipulators cocked at a curious angle, and Quilx'tch tried not to feel irritation as Ctx'qlt spread all eight limbs to their maximum extent in an exaggerated gesture of bewilderment.

"We did our best to hide the rope," Ctx'qlt raised a single manipulator to emphasize the singular nature of this rope in particular. "But I swear by the main swarm – the mother swarm – that they have some sort of instinct for finding exactly what you don't want them to find."

Quilx'tch wished for a moment that he could roll his eyes as the new commander, a young eager thing from the main university, tilted his head in curiosity.

"Which rope did the humans find?" the commander asked, folding his primary manipulators politely across his abdomen.

From the way the sensory hairs surrounding the commander's primary eyes bristled in confusion, Quilx'tch assumed that the question he really wanted to ask was if the quartermaster had seen the base psychologist recently.

"They – excuse me – Private Smith found the six centimeter diameter, soft-weave nanobot fiber rope. We had hidden the coil in the secondary storage container under the storm tarps."

Quilx'tch watched in amusement as the commander surreptitiously tapped out a note on his pad, a reminder to ask what storm tarps were. That particular horror could wait a bit longer according to the human meteorologists. At least there was an eighty percent chance it could.

"He said he was looking for a lighter," Ctx'qlt preemptively raised a manipulator to stop the commander from asking the question that was on his mandibles. "No, I don't know what a lighter is. He did not seem interested in enlightening me between his screams."

"Don't ask about the screams," Quilx'tch said softly.

The commander glanced at him uneasily but allowed the quartermaster to continue.

"He shifted the tarps," the quartermaster wrung his primary manipulators. "Do you have any idea how much they weigh? We have to get the entire swarm out to move one of those things."

The commander glanced at Quilx'tch, and Quilx'tch shook his head. That question didn't require an answer.

"So he moves the tarp," the quartermaster went on, "and found the rope, and it is the 'swimming hole' incident all over again." The quartermaster dropped his primary manipulators and looked at the commander expectantly. The commander gave Quilx'tch a rather desperate look, and the nutritional anthropologist took pity on the young officer. He raised one manipulator for attention.

"Pardon my intrusion," Quilx'tch asked. "How can this be a 'swimming hole' incident? The land around us is near uniformly flat at the humans' physical resolution, and none of the herbage around us is strong enough to provide the support for the rope."

The quartermaster expanded his mandibles as if to answer, but after a moment of hesitant clicking, he slumped. "Could you please just come outside and see for yourselves?" the quartermaster asked. "I just, we, we're not getting the safety award this cycle."

"Oh dear," Quilx'tch murmured as he gathered up his things. "We were on such a good track too. Our humans were being so reasonable."

He and the commander followed the quartermaster out of the conference room and then out of the main building. The 'screaming' became audible as soon as they passed the outer airlock along with the rumbling sound of one of the transport engines. They rounded the corner of the main building complex and stared in shock at the scene on the parking lot. One end of the rope had been secured in the clamp of the boom-claw used for taking samples. Apparently the device meant to reach far into underground caverns was strong enough to support both the rope and the human who was clinging to the lagging end. They had tied a knot in the end of the rope and were using this as a point to grip with the legs. The boom-claw was extended about four meters in the air and was slowly rotating, sending the human currently on the lagging end of the rope, Smith, Quilx'tch thought, swinging around in a wide circle. Another human was manipulating the boom-claw while the rest watched the action with wide grins of pleasure.

As the commander stared in stunned silence, the boom-claw stilled, and the humans leapt forward to stop the circular motion of their friend. Quilx'tch winced at the sound of two human bodies impacting, but neither seemed injured.

"Go, go, go!" the humans chanted.

Smith appeared to attempt a run for the main base building but staggered alarmingly to either side as if he had forgotten how to balance his precarious bipedal frame.

"Are they punishing him for some transgression?" the commander asked with just a touch of horror in the set of his legs.

"Given the fact that the rest of the humans are now competing to be the next one on the lagging end of the rope, probably not," the quartermaster pointed out.

Smith had collapsed on the ground and was laughing up at the sky as his friends abandoned him to claim a place on the rope. Quilx'tch took this to mean that he was out of the danger zone and led the commander over to the supine human.

"Friend Smith," Quilx'tch greeted the human, "may we climb on your chest?"

The human stopped laughing long enough to wave his hand in agreement before slipping his arms under his head and letting his gaze focus on the far distance that was so vague to Quilx'tch's people. *Was he cloud watching*? The commander looked like he had a thousand questions. The quartermaster looked like he was rather exasperated with all of the answers.

"What is it?" Quilx'tch asked after he had gotten Smith's attention by tapping his bristly chin. "What is it with humans and that rope?"

Humans are Weird – Pepper

"Who the flying flip keeps hiding the pepper?" Mack Dodge snarled out as he slammed the salt shaker onto the counter by the heating surface.

"Flying flip?" another human asked with a grin from where he sat, eating a bowl of oatmeal at the table.

"Headquarters says I need to share less cultural knowledge with this base," Mack said, rolling his eyes as he brought his plate of scrambled eggs to the table.

The dull gray wall of the makeshift kitchen crowded in over their heads. The Undulates had given the humans the largest storage bay on their base for this common space, but the breadbox-sized aliens had never built the structure with two-meter tall bipeds in mind. Mack sighed as he salted his eggs.

"Seriously, Bob," he said. "This is the third day running that the pepper has been missing."

"Eat oatmeal instead," Bob suggested with a grin.

Mack glared at him.

"Helping," Bob said in a singsong tone.

"Yesterday I found it in storage bay six," Mack continued as Bob returned to his oatmeal. "The day before that I found it with the lost and found box at the security desk."

"Well, I never touch the stuff," Bob pointed out. "Can't blame me."

"Well, there are only seven humans on this base," Mack

observed. "The pool of suspects is pretty small."

"There are forty-odd Undulates on the base however," Bob said.

"What would they want with our pepper?" Mack asked. "Piperine isn't technically a poison for them, but they don't go in for painful food."

The conversation was interrupted by a chime that announced the arrival of one of their hosts. Mack and Bob turned to glance at the small opening in the door that served the Undulates. The dusky red Undulate came in and waved his gripping appendages cheerfully at them.

"And what motile dust mop graces us with his presence today?" Bob asked cheerfully.

Mack winced at the sheer number of diplomatic regulations that question broke and not for the first time thanked heaven that the Undulates were so enthusiastic and forgiving.

"I am Spinsmadly," the Undulate replied. His tones were flat with effort. He had clearly learned human grammar but was still struggling with emotional expression. However, from the way his motile appendages jumped around under him, the Undulate was excited or agitated. "I am the quartermaster for the station and…" the Undulate hesitated, and the humans gave him time to work out his words. "I believe the proper translation is station safety officer."

"Well, hello then, Spinsmadly," Bob said, giving a wave. "How can we help you?"

"There has been a safety violation in this space for three days running," Spinsmadly said, arching his gripping appendages in a gesture that indicated either frustration or perplexity.

"Really now?" Bob asked, his grin spreading. "What violation was that?"

"I found raw ingredients for the non-lethal defense canisters next to the heating surface for food preparation," Spinsmadly said.

"And you moved them to a safer location?" Mack asked with a groan.

Spinsmadly stilled thoughtfully and then quickly scrambled to align himself towards the object of his attention, clearly remembering that humans were an aiming species. Bob burst out laughing.

"Have fun explaining why some humans eat pepper when the smart ones use it for a weapon," Bob said as he picked up his bowl and left the table.

"You eat raw piperine?" Spinsmadly asked Mack.

Mack tried not to laugh at how the quartermaster remembered halfway through the sentence to add tones of astonishment.

"It is called pepper when we dry and eat it," he said with a sigh.

This was going to be fun.

Humans Are Weird – Q-Tips

Everyone inhabiting Rough End Base knew that Thursdays were luxury days. Not every Thursday, mind, usually every third, but if the nebula were tricky, every fourth or fifth. The overworked Confederation supply ships rarely carried anything heavier than data in excess of the strictly necessary food and mechanical supplies. No, it was the cloud runners who brought the isolated sapients the little pleasures that saw them through the cold, dark nights and scorching days of a planet that just barely qualified as habitable.

"One box for Human Sharon," the Shatar free-merchant said, holding up a roughly rectangular box wrapped in brown paper.

At nearly two meters tall and covered in body paint and semi-precious stones, the outcast Shatar made a rather spectacular sight. The fact that there was no way to tell which of the ornaments were actually ornamental and which were weapons added a certain zest to these mostly legal transactions.

"Yes," Michael Sharon, PhD geology, crowed in delight as he snatched up the package. "About time."

"We brought it in good time," the Shatar said, his frill bristling with offense.

Sharon grinned at him and patted the free-merchant on what served him as a shoulder. "Sure thing, Big Guy," he assured the Shatar. "There is no question. Your little ships are never the problem. This probably got bogged down at the post office in Fairbanks."

The Shatar's skin or outer membrane – Sharon wasn't sure what exactly you called the smooth covering of their exoskeleton – cooled to a more reasonable shade of green. Or at least what was visible under the extensive body painting did. Big Guy dipped his antennae in curiosity even as he finished sorting the unclaimed packages back into his satchel. Sharon knew the free-merchant had a few hours before his ship had to jump back into the nebula currents and was probably interested in conversation. With a smile Sharon began to carefully open the paper wrapping that covered his purchase. Big Guy clicked in interest as he tilted his head back and forth to get a better look at the tightly packed items.

"Q-tips," Sharon explained as he popped the package open and pulled out two. He handed one to Big Guy and slipped the other into his ear with a contented sigh.

"What are you using that for?" Big Guy asked in surprise. "I was under the impression that human auditory canals were nearly as sensitive as our own."

"I'm cleaning out the waxy buildup in my ears," Sharon said with a grin. "It's okay. Look, there are instructions on the box."

Big Guy reached over and took the offered package. He held it up in front of his eyes and rolled his head to analyze the human writing.

"It says it is for applying dermal paint," Big Guy said in surprise. He glanced at the one in his hand and tested the soft tip with his fingers. He clicked in approval before turning back to the package. "It also says that it is good for cleaning hard surface optic sensors and applying medication to minor injuries." Big Guy's frill suddenly stiffened in a show of surprise, and he shot an annoyed and perplexed look at Sharon, who had taken a second Q-tip to his other ear. "And here... in markedly larger print... it specifically says that it is illegal, unsafe, and unsanitary to insert them in your ear canals. It says in fact that this behavior serves no purpose and causes damage."

"Does it now?" Sharon drawled, giving the Q-tip a twist.

Big Guy stared at him through one incredulous eye for a moment before tossing the package back and walking away, muttering something about humans.

Humans are Weird – Omnivorous

"So you just eat… anything?"

The breadbox-sized alien's vocal cords were perhaps the closest to a human's as any of the speaking species they had encountered. They tended to be quieter and pitched lower, but the one that Mack had dubbed Threes had learned to 'shout' early on and knew how to aim his words in the thin air.

"Well, not anything," Mack corrected as he tightened the bolts on the underside of the hover bike he was working on. "There are a lot of chemical compounds that are toxic in plants—"

"Of course there are," Threes said, exasperation tinting his voice. "It does not serve the plants' ends for you to devour their photosynthesis surfaces. They pump all sorts of anti-predation compounds into their energy-rich biomass!"

Mack heard the rustling that was the Undulate's version of footsteps, and the human couldn't resist a smile at the image of the giant caterpillar-like creature moving across the ground. Fortunately a species that expressed its chosen collective name as a rippling motion along the dreadlock-like appendages that seemed to compose the entirety of their bodies (that varied from individual to individual as well as from sub-culture to sub-culture) didn't mind getting 'named' by the other cultures they met.

"It is far safer to feed on the simpler creatures that the water is practically teeming with!" Threes made his way up onto Mack's chest, and Mack absently pushed him to a more comfortable position.

"Maybe safer," Mack agreed as he reached his hand deep into the guts of the machine. "But not as convenient. Not much of the human population lives with enough water to make that a viable option."

Threes clicked in distress and moved up Mack's chest to prod gently at his chin with – Mack assumed and hoped – his frontal appendages.

"But how?" Threes demanded.

Mack grunted and gave the hand signal for needing more information. Apparently human fingers were one of the best cross-species communication aids that the Undulates had ever discovered.

"Humans like water," Threes explained his query. "I know you don't live in it like we do, but you…" Mack assumed Threes was struggling with trying to communicate a complex Undulate word/position to someone who wasn't looking at him. "You swim and… and I think the closest word is wade… just like we do, and it is a valued exercise."

"Yup, we do love our bodies of water," Mack agreed as his hands finally found the loose nut he had been feeling around for. "Personally I grew up near Gitche Gumee. Went swimming a lot as a kid."

"But not everyone is so fortunate?" Threes pressed forward again, and Mack shoved him down again.

"Keep down for a while, Threes… I gotta get this loose. But yeah, some humans can go their entire lives without ever seeing enough standing water to wade in, let alone grow enough biomass to feed the population."

"Perhaps it has something to do with your fantastic biomass and nutrient needs," Threes suggested, trying to keep his voice level, but Mack could feel the Undulate shivering at the clearly horrible thought of desert living.

"Well, lots of folks even prefer it," Mack said with a grin.

"It certainly explains your dependence on omnivorous," Threes speculated.

"Omnivory," Mack corrected absently. Threes was particular about his languages and liked to get it right.

Humans Are Weird – Can't Sit Still

"Okay," Quilx'tch said, angling his eyes to stare at the human who was crouched in the corner bent over his computer. Bill was wrapped in a blanket, and his entire body was making a series of small, sustained jerking moments. "Bill is ill. But why isn't he resting in bed?"

"Eh," the healthy human continued to boil the 'chicken soup' on the small camp stove. "Bill just is one of those humans who can't sit still."

"But sitting still is how you conserve energy to heal," Quilx'tch said slowly, trying to find the point in this conversation that was keeping him from understanding the situation rather than illuminating it.

"Soup's ready," the cook said cheerfully, abandoning the attempt. "Ready to take your sample?"

"Indeed," Quilx'tch held up the sample container in his foremost legs. "And this 'chicken soup' has healing properties?"

"Maybe," the cook shrugged. "It will make him feel better."

Quilx'tch filed that thought away and skittered back to his lab. He had learned that sick humans didn't always like company, and he did not know Bill well enough to confidently offer it. He would do his own job in analyzing this foodstuff and would pass on this strange, counterproductive behavior to the behavioral anthropologists.

Humans are Weird – Inanimate Objects

"Quilx'tch, can you aid me?"

Quilx'tch glanced over at his superior as he entered the room. The chief cultural anthropologist was crouched over the main data screen in their office. Quilx'tch balanced the vials in his manipulators and rotated uneasily.

"Can it wait a moment, Tca'kct?" he replied. "I need to place the samples from the Hellbats in the refrigerator."

"Make sure you place them in the sample refrigerator," Tca'kct reminded him sternly. "But yes, that will be acceptable."

Quilx'tch rotated and hurried to put the nutrient samples in the racks of the refrigeration unit. He made sure their labels were clearly visible and scurried back to where Tca'kct was flicking various symbols across the visual display screen. Quilx'tch aligned his primary eyes with the screen and tilted his abdomen to the side thoughtfully.

"Is this one of those human word puzzles?" he asked.

Tca'kct let out a chitter of irritation and swept a primary manipulator across the control surface, realigning the letters in the orderly rows the humans preferred.

"Betty," Quilx'tch read. "A common derivate of a human name, female, I believe."

"Yes, yes," Tca'kct said. "I am aware of that. However, the base command transport has no sex so far as I know."

Quilx'tch let his secondary eyes take in the stressed commander. Had he been getting sufficient nutrients lately? In lieu of a proper field medic, it was Quilx'tch's task to ensure the base crew maintained their health.

"Oh, swarm," Tca'kct snapped his mandibles at Quilx'tch. "Do stop thinking so loudly. I am fine."

"You know your inappropriate use of that term has the humans thinking we are telepathic," Quilx'tch reprimanded him.

"I take zero responsibility for what humans think," Tca'kct said. "Now this," he waved at the offending female name, "this is exactly why Mechanic Steve has named the command transport Betty."

Quilx'tch felt his joints loosen with relief. "Oh, yes, they do that," he said. "The transports that drop off the humans are in fact listed by their 'names' rather than their identification numbers in the files for the foodstuffs."

"I am aware, Quilx'tch," Tca'kct said, rubbing the ridges over his eyes. "If you read the functional briefing on humans, it lists that facet of their behavior. It also lists that that only refers to ships of a certain mass."

"I was not aware of that," Quilx'tch said.

"But Mechanic Steve has named a wheeled vehicle far below the tonnage requirements Betty," Tca'kct said.

"I assume you have tried simply asking him," Quilx'tch said.

"He muttered something inaudible and walked away after I asked why he had given an inanimate object a name," Tca'kct replied. "Since then, I have been operating under the assumption that it is some form of what the humans call an acronym."

"Well," Quilx'tch began to back slowly away, "I will get back to my nutrient analysis."

"One day we will understand the humans," Tca'kct muttered to himself as he bent back over the control panel. "One day."

Quilx'tch made a mental note to check on Tca'kct's nutrient intake. Sometimes odd behavior was explainable by poor diet. On another leg, sometimes it was just prolonged exposure to humans.

Humans are Weird – Seeds

Quilx'tch woke to a very peculiar grinding noise. He shook off the foggy webs of sleep and slipped out from under the 'comforter' that his particular human friend on his last posting had made him and walked to the edge of his bunk. He rotated his primary eyes to locate the source of the sound. Perhaps unsurprisingly it was coming from his current roommate. A young human with decidedly unhealthy sleep habits. Said human was currently sitting hunched in front of a projected display that appeared to be other humans in a large city of sorts. The grinding sound appeared to be coming from his mouth.

Quilx'tch felt his sensory hairs perk with interest. "What are you eating, Scotty?" Quilx'tch asked eagerly.

"Just some almonds," Scotty replied, absently holding out one hand, palm up to display several tapered ovaloids. "I wanted some protein to see me through this episode."

"I have never seen this food source," Quilx'tch said, scurrying along the shelf that wrapped around their room so that he paused just over the proffered food.

"Sure you have," Scotty said. "The cook puts them in the smoothies all the time. Great source of protein."

Quilx'tch clicked in confirmation and carefully picked up the surprisingly heavy object. He clicked in surprise as he examined it. "Pardon me, Scotty," Quilx'tch said, "but is this a dormant-stage seed?"

"The almonds?" Scotty replied. "I guess so. I think they come from trees."

"Trees," Quilx'tch said a bit flatly. "You are eating unprocessed, dormant-stage tree seeds?"

Scotty looked at him curiously. "Yeah, so?"

Quilx'tch pondered how to phrase his question. "Exactly how much pressure are your jaws capable of producing?"

"Scratch if I know," Scotty said.

Quilx'tch flexed his gripping appendages over the hard mass of biomatter, calculating how much power it must take to grind the seed into the requisite paste humans preferred to digest. A tiny shiver ran over his carapace at the thought of that destructive power. It was probably a good thing their mouth openings were so small. Still there was a wealth of knowledge to be gained here. Such destructive force must leave telltale signs on the human's bodies. He might even be able to use those signs to determine a method for figuring out human diet just from observing these patterns.
Fascinating.

Humans are Weird – Report

Report from Cultural Researcher Qulix'tch to Home Swarm University – Re: Human Survival Rates As it Relates To Diet

Dearest colleagues,

I am ever grateful for your kind communications and support. I have compiled all collected data and attached it to the overview for your perusal. Let me say first and foremost that the rumors that I was sent to investigate, i.e., that humans were the first observed truly omnivorous species, have turned out to be a gross understatement.

It is not simply that humans can eat both vegetative flesh and animal flesh, not even that they can eat anything in between, but seriously, they eat everything regardless of its inherent nutrient value and risk factor. Indeed this increases their odds of survival, but from an intercultural interaction standpoint, it is a little weird and creepy – let's be honest – that it seems like their first thought when encountering something new that isn't a rock is "Can I eat this?"

Mostly they prefer plant matter (thank whatever deity you will) as they seem to be squeamish about eating sentient beings, and the odds favor that plants won't be. It has also come to my attention that our particular eight-legged and multi-eyed form, added to our chitinous outer membrane, is particularly unappetizing to them across their multi-culture. This is reassuring but hardly a firm deterrent as they have an instinct set that drives them to make digestible anything that isn't inherently.

The nutrients are trapped in an unusable form? No worries; the human just finds something combustible, builds a fire, and heats it till the indigestible fibers or whatever release the nutrients.

Is the edible bit protected by spikes, spines, and thorns? They might just grab a rock and beat it until the edible bit is available.

They carry around vats of acid just in case they need to add it to the mix to denature large proteins.

I kid you not; they have hundreds, *hundreds*, of different species of microbes on their skin, in their mouth, in their digestive tract that help them break down what their own systems won't.

If the nutrients are contaminated with unfriendly microorganisms, they count on this friendly micro-fauna, as they call it, to fight them off. Failing that, they have developed an entire subculture devoted to brewing poison of just the correct potency that it kills the intruding microorganisms while leaving them alive.

And if there is no plant matter they can eat? They just find a (hopefully) non-sentient species that can break it down for them and wring the proteins and nutrients out of them in ways that don't bear mentioning. (See appendix Eggs, Milk, and Meat.)

It has been reported, if you can believe it (and with humans, why not), that on their own planet, in an ocean that is full of fish that they can eat with no processing at all, there is one species that is particularly poisonous to humans. Instead of avoiding it and eating the swarming fish species that are so benign that they can be eaten without even the basic heating, humans pay to have a specialist in food preparation known as a chef go through a complicated ritual to remove the deadly toxin. They will do this even when the non-toxic fish flesh is readily and far more cheaply available.

Then, even when they have enough nutrients, they will masticate whatever inorganic substance is at hand in some odd, seemingly unconscious ritual. The humans I encountered seemed to have a preference for writing utensils for this purpose.

I hope the information I have gathered will prove useful.

Humans are Weird – Insecticide

"So to my understanding," Mother of Half said carefully, the human language falling from her mandibles with difficultly, "you are going to kill the chitinous life forms that are eating our tree crops with... music?"

"Well, it is more like sounds harmonized exactly to the frequencies that will drive them out of the host trees, and it won't directly kill them, but that is the general idea and result," Ranger Mack assured her.

Mother of Half stared at him intently with her forward-facing predatory eyes, and her neck frill rose and fell in concentration while her antennae twitched.

"Oh," Mack said, pausing in tuning the device in question. "On another note… are you going to be coming to the sing-along at the community center tomorrow?"

She paused and ran her fingers over the chitinous membrane that covered her arm. "I'll think about it, Friend Human," she said. "I'll think about it."

Humans are Weird – Shots

"Yeah, just got the call, I'm needed down in the engine compartment, so sorry, later."

Fourth Sister stared blankly out after the back of the retreating human as she tried to process the suddenly empty medical bay. She clicked her mandibles thoughtfully and placed the syringe back in the sterile cabinet she had drawn it from. She lifted her hand to the comm unit on the wall and activated it.

"Chief Engineer," she said crisply, "this is Chief Medic."

After a moment, the device chimed. "Yes?" the cheerful answer came back.

"Did you summon Fifth Engineer to aid you?" Fourth Sister asked.

"Fifth? Oh, you mean Robinson?" Chief Engineer asked. "No. He's scheduled for a medbay visit today, according to the chart. Why?"

"He just left the medical bay in a state of agitation, citing the necessity of his presence in engineering," she explained.

"Well, that's weird," Chief Engineer muttered. "Was he done with his treatment?"

"No!" Fourth Sister snapped. "In fact I was just about to administer—" She cut herself off, remembering the humans' restriction on medical information, but Chief Engineer burst out laughing.

"You were about to administer his nutrient shot," he surmised. "Yeah, he's scared of needles. You'll have to track him down and basically drag him back to the medbay for that."

"Human law does not allow for forced medical treatment," Fourth Sister pointed out.

"You won't have to force him," Chief Engineer assured her. "This is literally a do-or-die situation. Tell you what. I'll have Jonsey drag him back and sit him in the chair. Oh yeah, be prepared for him to pass out. Safety restraints might be a good idea."

Fourth Sister clasped her mandibles together and laid her frill back against her head. There was so much wrong in that statement she didn't know where to start.

"How precisely," she finally asked, "is Second Navigator going to capture and return him to the medical bay? She is perhaps a fourth of his mass."

"I told you," Chief Engineer said cheerfully. "It's not a matter of force. She's the best to convince him."

"I have seen Fifth Engineer walk into the medical bay," Fourth Sister said thoughtfully, "under his own power with a handspan of cryo-steel lodged into his thigh. He was laughing over it."

"So?" Chief Engineer asked.

"Why is he afraid of a sterile subdermal needle to the point that safety restraints are necessary?" Fourth Sister demanded.

"Spike me if I know," Chief Engineer said cheerfully. "Phobias aren't supposed to make sense. There we go. Jonsey says she caught him in the cafeteria, and she'll have him back in your seat in two shakes of a cat's tail. Cheers and remember the restraints."

The comm chimed off, and Fourth Sister lowered her hand. She drew in a long breath and released it. *Humans.*

Humans are Weird – Crystals

"Twistunder?"

The breadbox-sized alien slumped in frustration as he turned his attention away from his report for the forty-second time this day.

"Yes, Spinsinagitation?" he replied, being careful to modulate his body language calmly. It wasn't Spinsinagitation's fault that the base was full of humans. "What do you need?"

"I have a question," Spinsinagitation asked. His hesitation was painfully obvious in the meticulous way that his appendages lifted and dropped. "It is about the human's behavior."

"Of course it is," Twistunder said. At least the subangles suggested it was only one human the younger Undulate was asking about. He waited for the question.

"There are crystals hanging in the base windows," Spinsinagitation finally began.

"Yes," Twistunder said with stiffer movements than he intended to. "Humans are unable to discern differentiation in solar light. Each sun has a single color to their eyes. The crystals are for ornamentation. They scatter the light so the humans can see a broader range of the spectrum."

"Yes," Spinsinagitation waved his gripping appendages quickly. "That was in the briefing file. I had a chance to observe a human without him knowing I was there."

Twistunder pulled his appendages under him in anticipation. This was going to be good.

"It was the solar angle of optimum light scattering," Spinsinagitation explained. "What the informational packet called a full seven. And Human Steve was in the white room. The central foci of the refractions were moving over the walls of the room due to the crystal swinging, and Human Steve was… was…" The younger Undulate paused, and his appendages dropped in frustration. "I think he was hunting the foci?"

"Hunting," Twistunder replied stiffly. "Hunting the foci."

"Yes…" Spinsinagitation started again. "He was… creeping around the room, following the refraction foci… the rainbows, they call them, I think… then every time he was close to one, he would… I think the word is 'pounce.' He pounced on them, grasping the flat wall with his primary appendages. Then he would… grin… I believe the word is… and start stalking another one. Then… then the crystal stopped moving, and the foci stopped moving, and he frowned and walked over and nudged the crystal to start the foci moving again."

Spinsinagitation stopped and drooped in perplexity, his primary gripping appendages lifted in supplication to Twistunder. The older Undulate twitched and thought longingly of his report.

"I don't know, Spins," Twistunder said with a droop. "I just don't know."

Humans are Weird – Cold Sores

"Yeah, so I'm pretty sure from what the medical computer says that this won't be contagious, but it's a viral outbreak, and I don't know whether my implant works on skin conditions like this."

Quilx'tch stood behind his commander as they listened to the slightly slurred voice of the audio-only communication coming from the human who had locked himself in his quarters. The nutritional anthropologist was concerned. Any time the term 'viral outbreak' was used, it was time for concern. But the human had willingly isolated himself and was, after all, human. It wasn't like they were so fragile as to be taken out by their own internal microbes. He thought, hoped.

He signaled his approval of the course of action to the commander but held up one leg to stop him before the formal order was given.

"You mentioned that the symptom was visible on your face?" Quilx'tch asked. "This 'cold sore.'"

"Yeah, Quick," the human responded. "It's a doozy too."

"A doozy?" Quilx'tch asked.

"Especially big and red," the human explained.

Quilx'tch clicked in confirmation and rubbed his primary manipulators together, trying not to sound too eager, but the human seemed to hear it anyway. The human laughed.

"Do you really want to see it, Quick?" he asked.

"It would be for science," Quilx'tch insisted, but he could not restrain the eagerness in his voice. "These types of surface irritations are rare among chitinous species like ours for the mere reason that they can so easily be fatal and—"

His voice cut off, and he bristled in horror as the human activated the visual connection. The human blinked in surprise, and his face broke into an amused grin.

"Y'all're so cute when ya puff up like that," the human said.

"You are bleeding," the commander said, his legs tight with disgust and fear. "You smiled, and now you are bleeding from your mandibles."

"Lips," the human corrected, idly reaching up to dab at the blood and puss leaking from the lesion on his skin. "My mandible is inside, and I only have one."

"Pustule is covering nearly twenty percent of your visible endothelial surface," Quilx'tch said when he could finally bring himself to speak.

"Yeah," the human squinted at him in bland confusion as he replied. "If you say so, I guess. I figured this'd freak you little guys out. You know... cuz your exoskeleton integrity is so important to you. It's why I decided to stay in till this healed. Suggested protocol from the Ranger Core."

Quilx'tch quickly drew himself up into a less horrified stature. "Yes, yes, and as I recall, human surface damage is not nearly so hazardous. So you are quite well? I can't bring you anything to aid your recovery from the galley?"

"Well, some of those fresh berries would be nice," the human admitted. "Fresh fruit always has been a Navy man's best friend."

"I will pick some myself immediately," Quilx'tch said, backing out of the room. "The commander can finish the communication."

He was well aware that he had left the room with less dignity than he had ever possessed, but he felt no qualms about leaving that revolting sight to the commander. He shuddered from hair tip to hair tip. Cold sores. Oh dear, this was going to be a report and a half.

Humans are Weird – Petting It

The setting red sun caught in every branch of the primordial forest and cast its diffused glow on the already red fur of Prince Triclick. He was currently adjusting a milky white apron so it sat more easily over his wings. His companion, half his size and several shades lighter, not to mention bearing none of the battle scars that crossed and reclosed Triclick's war-worn flesh, gazed at him with skepticism pouring out of his beady, black eyes.

"You," the flight second said, "you are going to be a nurse?"

Triclick hissed in passive irritation as he pulled out a tin of polish to add a little scented shine to his three remaining sensory horns and ease the ever-present pain in the five stumps. "No," he said firmly. "I am simply volunteering my off hours to give aid and comfort to our allies who have sacrificed so much to our cause."

"Oh, I would never question how much we owe the humans," the flight second said grimly. "Granted, they gained from this campaign too, but we would have never reclaimed this world without them."

"So you sound my depth," Triclick said. His voice distorted slightly as he examined his teeth, still needle sharp, he thought proudly, in the reflection on the back of his tin.

"They call us Hellbats," the flight second said bluntly. "I have seen humans who have been allies for months burst out screaming when a flight breaks from the ground in front of them. We literally," he held up his wing claws for emphasis, "resemble nothing so much as the messengers of their underworld."

82

"Your point?" Triclick asked blandly as he checked his appearance one more time.

"What," the flight second demanded, "in the name of the First Flight makes you think that the presence of our most feared warrior would offer injured humans any comfort at all? Most likely they will just sit there in mortal terror and fear of offending you."

"One would think," Triclick admitted. "But that has not been the result observed by the medics."

Before the flight second could respond, Triclick leapt off of the branch they had perched on and flew in lazy spirals towards the tent on the forest floor marked with a bold red cross. The flight second hissed and followed him. However, there was no chance to begin the conversation again before they fluttered to a stop outside of the insect-repelling netting. They slipped through the barrier and landed on the massive desk that served the human medics. The one on duty smiled up at them from his paperwork and waved them in.

There was only one human in the medical ward today the flight second saw. A young human, one of the new batch, he supposed. From the pale tint of his face and the audible gurgling from his abdomen, he had been bedridden for some digestive malady. The flight second grimaced, but Prince Triclick flew fearlessly up to the human and landed on the edge of the bed. As the flight second had expected, the human started violently at seeing Triclick.

"Greetings, Friend Smithson!" Triclick said, dipping his head as he landed. "Are you ready to begin your therapy again?"

To the flight second's surprise, the agitation almost immediately left the human's face, and he nodded eagerly.

"Sure thing, Commander—" the human began.

"Ah, stt," Triclick hissed in remonstrance.

"Right, right, no ranks in here," the human said with a laugh.

"'One mustn't offend the medics,'" Triclick quoted in all seriousness. "Now, let's begin." He hopped over and lay flat out on a blanket that covered the human's knee. The human reached out a hand hesitantly and then gently lowered it to stroke the exposed length of fur between Triclick's scarred wings. The flight second watched in astonishment as the human relaxed back against his pillows with a happy sigh as he continued stroking the fourth in line to the throne.

"Now, where was I?" Prince Triclick began when the human seemed to have achieved a proper pace. "Ah, yes, Five Trills and the Second Prince of the Golden Cliffs. Now it was the latter days of the great migration."

The flight second blinked in astonishment for a moment, then shook his head. Triclick had always been a bit of an odd one. But how was he going to explain this in his report? One didn't just upend two decades of xeno-psychology research with a field note that says, *And they like petting furry things.*

Humans are Weird – Massage

"Security! Security!" the frantic voice of one of the winged species echoed over the comms, high and piercing.

Under normal circumstances, the Shatar currently at the security desk would have found the tones annoying as it echoed off of his frill and gave him a pounding headache. He idly wondered if skulls made of true bone resounded less to high frequency noise. Today of all days, this forty-second interruption of his office duties made him want to sic his blessed grandmothers on the irritating little scientist.

"There is a medical emergency in the human's quarters," the flitting little scamp cried out.

A horrible, low moan of pain filled the sound waves over and around the high frequency language of the Hellbats. Oh, how he wanted to dismiss the interruption with a click of his mandibles. However, there were rules and regulations for a reason. This might be different than every other call today. It might actually be a medical emergency unrelated to the sounds.

"Please give me the details," he said curtly.

"There are the most horrible groaning and howling noises coming from the secondary work room," the Hellbat declared.

The Shatar on security duty rubbed the ridges around his faceted eyes with a sigh and carefully took the details. When he had enough and the Hellbat paused, he interjected quickly.

"These sounds have already been investigated and explained," the Shatar clicked out. "The humans are performing a medical relaxation ceremony to disrupt the buildup of," he checked the notes the human medical professional had given him, "lactic acid in their muscles. They have assured me the sounds are a necessary part of the massage."

There was almost a pause as the Hellbat considered his words. "Did they run out of painkillers?" the Hellbat asked. "Do they need us to fire up the chemical mixers?"

"It was explained to me," the Shatar said, "that the procedure not only required full sensory alertness but that it was… in totality… pleasurable."

"So will this be going on for some time?" the Hellbat asked cautiously.

"Several more hours," the Shatar said grimly. "Each human apparently gets a turn under the care of the masseuse."

"It is a lovely day outside," the Hellbat offered. "I think the flight will rest out in the forest."

"There is a small camp set up out there already," the Shatar stated with a sigh. "I am the only non-human left in the base."

"Hopefully your office is soundproofed," the Hellbat said before signing off without using the proper procedure.

"It is," the Shatar muttered to himself. "Now if only no more concerned crewmates open the comm lines."

Humans are Weird – Clicker

"Be careful!" Quilx'tch called out.

Called out too late, he realized sadly as the delicate sample container fell out of his assistant's manipulators, rolled to the edge of the work surface, and teetered for a moment on the edge of the abyss. It caught the diffuse light of the lab one last time and fell over the edge to shatter on the floor.

"I am sorry!" his assistant blurted out. "Oh, we only have two left after this. I am so sorry."

"Still your mandibles," Quilx'tch said, letting his thorax slump to the floor. "I should have secured it to the wall. This is my responsibility."

His assistant was still keeping his legs tight to his body in a display of stress.

"Please relax," Quilx'tch said, reaching over to stroke his assistant's dorsal line. "This is just the sort of thing you have to learn to deal with when working on human-sized bases."

"We will have to clean up the broken shards," his assistant said so quietly Quilx'tch barely concealed it.

"Yes, best do that before the human sees the—" Quilx'tch began.

"Hey, lil buddies!" a third voice startled them. "I heard a crash. Everything okay?"

"I dropped a large sample container," the assistant said, raising his voice so the human could hear him.

"Ah!"

The human's face suddenly lit up with pleasure. Quilx'tch refused to let his legs tighten in irritation. He could sense the confusion in his assistant but didn't bother explaining. The consequences would become obvious soon enough.

"Was it one of the ones with the pressure-sensing lids?" the human asked eagerly.

"It was," the assistant confirmed.

"And you can't use the tops on other containers, right?" the human continued.

"That is true," the assistant said. "We will recycle it."

"Can I have it then?" the human asked. "I'll help you clean up the mess."

"I see no issue with that arrangement," the assistant said eagerly, "if you have a use for it." The assistant turned to Quilx'tch, and his mentor waved a manipulator in acceptance.

"Sweet!" the human began to bustle around the room, cleaning up the shattered container.

"What does he need the pressure sensor for?" the assistant asked Quilx'tch.

"Ask him yourself," Quilx'tch suggested as he turned back to his work. "I am going to fetch a new container and the securing cables."

The assistant approached the edge of the work surface and called out to the human. "What are you going to use the pressure sensor for?" the assistant asked.

The human grinned down at the assistant while dumping the shards into a recycling container. He lifted up the lid; the entire thing fit easily across two of the human's fingers. He placed his thumb on the mechanical pressure sensor and depressed it with a loud click. The assistant tilted his head to the side in confusion. The human grinned and began depressing the sensor rapidly. The assistant stared in confusion at the clearly amused human for some time before speaking again.

"Why are you doing that?" he asked.

"It's fun!" the human said brightly. "I used to have one of these as a kid. Got it off a drink bottle. Thanks again, little bud."

The human strolled out, whistling and followed by a rapid-fire clicking. The assistant turned back to where Quilx'tch was wrestling the new container into place.

"Don't ask me," Quilx'tch said. "Now come help me secure this one."

Humans Are Weird – Sweat

"Excuse me, Friend Dodge," the voice came from behind him, startling the Ranger from his brown study of the remaining miles of moon-like terrain they faced.

"Yes, Fif-Friend Fifty-seven Clicks?" he replied, just remembering to add in the honorific. Not that he minded. Once you had shared a malfunctioning ship, a landing that was not a crash by a margin of a few meters per second, and the news that you were going to have to hoof (or wing in his friend's case) it forty miles across a featureless desert to the nearest supply cache, there was no reason not to call each other friends. A ginger blur came around and focused into a fluttering bat-like creature.

"I suspect that your water supply is leaking," Fifty-seven Clicks informed him with his horrifyingly adorable face scrunched up in what Mack Dodge had learned was a sign of distress.

Mack grunted, stood immediately, and began to shrug off his backpack. The partial shade that the rock outcropping had offered only covered him if he was sitting, but this needed attention now.

"Well, let's see," Mack muttered, carefully examining the mouthpiece, the tube that led to the main reservoir in his pack, and then the reservoir itself. "I can't see or feel anything wrong with it, and it doesn't look like I've lost any water," Mack finally said. "What makes you think it's leaking?"

"You are covered in water, Friend Dodge!" Fifty-seven Clicks insisted. Mack heard the fluttering of leathery wings and felt a velvet brush against his back before the Itsy-Bitsy Hellbat flew around to his face and held up a dripping wet manipulating claw. "Look at this!"

"That's just sweat," Mack said with a sigh, slinging his pack back on and securing the buckles. "Come on... I've rested enough. Let's get going. I want to make another ten miles before we make camp."

"What is sweat, and where is it coming from if not your water reservoir?" Fifty-seven Clicks demanded, fluttering around in front of Mack, his dusky ginger fur catching the dim light of the three suns.

"Did you read the section in our briefing about how humans achieve thermoregulation?" Mack asked ruefully, already knowing the answer.

"No," Fifty-seven Clicks replied without any seeming embarrassment.

Mack sighed and shook his head as he started out. "I have a set of glands that pumps water out from my internal reserves, and then my skin uses the resulting temperature drop due to evaporation to pull the heat away from my internals and radiate it out into the surrounding atmosphere." Maybe not the most accurate summation, but internal biology wasn't really his specialty.

He hoped he was mostly accurate because Fifty-seven Clicks was so stunned by this revelation that he waited for what must have been a full five seconds before replying. "The amount of water you must have to store would be enormous!" he chattered out excitedly.

"I'm ninety percent water," Mack commented though his training suggested this might not be strictly relevant.

"That is a lot of weight!" Fifty-seven Clicks still seemed shocked. "Just to carry around and expend like that."

"Legs," Mack indicated the limbs in question. "They are really good for carrying extra weight."

"It just seems inefficient," Fifty-seven Clicks commented.

"Well, we can't all have sensory horns that double as thermoregulators," Mack said philosophically.

"They are very useful," Fifty-seven Clicks agreed, hovering to preen the organs in question. His four (rightly two and a half) sets marked him as rather young, but they were quite a source of pride to him.

Mack grinned and gave a chuckle. It was going to be a long walk, and he was glad Fifty-seven Clicks was in a good mood.

Humans Are Weird – Fireworks

"Quilx'tch?"

The voice sounded from around the wall of the office, and the nutritional anthropologist clicked out a response absently. The speaker fluttered into the room and came to rest across from the console where three of Quilx'tch's eight legs were rapidly tapping away at the screen.

"Quilx'tch…" the Hellbat began, his fur flat in some uneasy emotion.

Quilx'tch twitched in irritation and raised his primary eyes to focus on the base safety officer. "Can I aid you, Five Clicks?" Quilx'tch asked. He had more experience than most at fighting the instinctual fear his species had of the Hellbats, but it was still uncomfortable to be in the same room with one.

"How did you know that I should not have approved the cultural display today?" Five Clicks demanded in a rush, his sensory horns dull with inattention.

Quilx'tch paused and pondered the question. "I did not know exactly," he said carefully. "I simply noted that the humans were 'grinning' and 'snickering' and 'giggling' all together."

"Those are supposed to be an indication of pleasure and comfort!" Five Clicks hissed.

"Indeed," Quilx'tch said, backing up a bit. "However, my personal observations have indicated that if all three of those factors occur simultaneously, then the possibility that the humans are involved in some form of dangerous mischief is high."

Five Clicks gave a whistling moan and covered his sensory horns with his wings, giving the horns an absent rub.

"There is also an informal rule I found in a cache of human documents," Quilx'tch continued. "At the time I assumed it was a jest, but perhaps it was in earnest after all."

"What rule?" Five Clicks asked without looking up from under his wings.

"If the thought of something makes an adult human giggle for more than fifteen seconds, it should not be allowed," Quilx'tch replied.

A sudden explosion rumbled through the base, and Quilx'tch gripped the console in fear.

"What did you let them do?" he demanded when Five Clicks didn't respond to the noise with anything other than a full frame shudder.

"Fireworks," Five Clicks hissed. "They are displaying fireworks."

Humans are Weird – Contagious Behavior

"The humans are a terrible influence on the Undulates!" Forty-seven Clicks spat out as he fluttered to a landing beside Quilx'tch.

"Oh really?" Quilx'tch asked as he adjusted his foot coverings over locomotion legs for the fifth time that day. "I hadn't noticed."

The Hellbat glared at him though narrow eyes. "How can you not have noticed!" Forty-seven Clicks hissed out. "I know for a fact that those contraptions are for keeping that surfactant off of your skin!"

"Exoskeleton," Quilx'tch corrected him. "And I was attempting to use sarcasm."

"Oh, please don't," groaned the Hellbat. "I don't think I can stand any more human madness spreading to other species today."

Quilx'tch didn't bother apologizing. Both he and his colleague were all too aware of the general rule that strongly dissuaded them from actively discouraging play between the species after work, and there was no doubt that the humans and Undulates were having a blast playing with the new toy the humans had introduced.

"I am going out to observe the situation," Quilx'tch stated grimly. "Do you wish to assist me?"

"There is no way," Forty-seven Clicks hissed, "that I am going out there until this is over. You land-bound folk cannot understand."

Quilx'tch wished for a moment he could roll his eyes. Having eight of them would no doubt make the gesture even more meaningful, but he satisfied himself with bristling his hair and stalking out. It was a fairly long walk from his office to the ponds where the Undulates and humans recreated, but long before he got there, the foot coverings were serving their purpose as he avoided the sticky patches on the ground. He flinched back as his eyes caught and magnified the glistening 'bubble' that floated over his head, but he soldiered on gamely. Soon the sound of laughing and trilling met his ears, and he hurried forward to the safe tree that had been set up near the ponds for his use. The grips were mostly sticky with the residue of the humans' game, but he managed to find a secure perch as he observed the game in progress.

A few of the humans stood at one end of the pond, using the directional force of their mammalian lungs to 'blow' atmosphere through soap-covered loops. This formed the 'bubbles' that drifted on the wind over the pond. In the water, the majority of the Undulates were frisking about at their maximum speed, chasing the bubbles. A few Undulates had take up the bubble wands and were vigorously waving them over their bodies in an attempt to form the bubbles. The crowd rumbled with every known sign of delight and pleasure for the two species.

Quilx'tch shuddered and crept closer to the trunk of the tree as one of the bubbles drifted close to him. He saw his own eight eyes reflected in an opalescent ghost and fought the urge to flee in panic. *Understanding differences is why I am out here instead of with my home swarm,* he reminded himself firmly. *The humans are enjoying themselves, and I will figure out why.*

Humans are Weird – Downgrade

"Maria, I will need assistance in the astrometrics department tomorrow," Fourth Sister said as she passed the communal room.

Several seconds passed with no response from the human who was sprawled out on the Shatarian couch. Fourth Sister tilted her head to the side in irritation. She understood that human joints didn't bend the same way as hers did, but was it truly more comfortable for them to spread out from the floor to the back of the couch in that almost Undulate manner? They did have an internal skeleton after all. They should act like it.

"Maria," Fourth Sister attempted again but with no better results. "Dr. Torres!" Deciding that she wasn't going to get any response through sound, Fourth Sister reached back and unlimbered her utility rod from its sheath on her back. She eased up to within a length of the couch and lightly rapped an exposed elbow.

Maria yelped and scrambled onto the floor. She blinked her odd concentric eyes at Fourth Sister and bared her blocky, enameled mandibles in a friendly gesture. Her fibrous frill was formed into twin braids that almost mimicked proper Shatarian frills from the southern fens. She had even thoughtfully added bright red ribbons to show her general placid attitude.

"What's up, Sis?" Maria asked brightly, pulling her headphones back.

"I will need your assistance tomorrow," Fourth Sister repeated, laying her frill back carefully to conceal her irritation. It was Maria's day off after all. "The final decision on star cluster radius has come down, and we will need to update the star maps that are not directly connected to the main systems and any printed data."

"Cool, gotcha!" Maria said brightly as she leapt to her feet.

Fourth Sister had to fight back another wince as the human towered over her. It was odd, going from the tallest species in the confederation to the second tallest; odd and unnerving.

"Would you like preference on the printer for personal reasons?" Fourth Sister asked.

"Why would I need that?" Maria asked in confusion.

"This is not your regular duty," Fourth Sister replied. "The base commander likes to make sure that anyone asked to perform outside of their job description gets some reimbursement even if it is minor."

"I know that," Maria said with a dismissive wave. "But why would I need access to the printer?"

"Nearly three quarters of the wall decorations in your room will need to be updated," Fourth Sister pointed out. "Ah! Perhaps you did not realize the decision will affect the Polaris system."

Maria fell silent, and Fourth Sister had to twist her head several times to analyze the wild flush of colors that rushed across the human's face.

"Are you ill, Maria?" she demanded, feeling her frill flatten with concern. "Did you get up too fast?"

Maria snapped her head from side to side, and Fourth Sister had to remind herself that it was a sign of negation rather than a request for more information. Maria's fleshy mammalian lips opened and closed a few times, and then the colors in her face suddenly cooled.

"They are reclassifying the Polaris system to what?" she finally hissed out.

Anger. Fourth Sister suddenly realized. That widely diffused anger that had no target and left humans so unpredictable. She frantically tried to figure out what had triggered this response in the normally gentle and merry human.

"They simply clarified that the outer two stars are not a part of the core system, making the actual system a tertiary," Fourth Sister answered the obvious question.

"What!" Maria demanded, her voice hitting an octave that Mother of Eighth used to sterilize the grain crops back home. Fourth Sister tried to repeat the information, but the human interrupted her. "They cut off the fifth little piggy?" Maria demanded. "Not just the fifth, the fourth too? Oh, sweet stars above, this is preposterous! That has always been a five-star system. Think of how many times I chanted that song as I skipped rope. Think of all the babies' toes that were pinched to the rhyme!"

She slapped her hands together and stalked out of the communal room.

"Oh, the Central University is going to hear about this!" was the last thing that Fourth Sister heard as the human left.

She stared blankly at the door and realized she was holding her datapad in front of her defensively. She carefully lowered it and just as carefully raised her frill into a calm position. All evidence indicated that Maria was furious over a technical designation change on an uninhabited system, but that could not be correct. It was patently illogical. She would call her cousin who lived on the mixed colony. If anyone could explain this behavior, it was a Shatar who had to deal with these strange beings her entire life.

Humans are Weird – Fist Bump

"I doubt the trade agreements will change much in the next two days," Tca'sk said as he adjusted his perch on his human friend's shoulder. "It is a holiday for the Shatar, and the human offices are going to be focused on restructuring their computer servers."

"You are probably right," Damian muttered.

After this short response, he went back to chewing gently on his lower lip. A fascinating habit that Tca'sk was glad he had a chance to observe closely. It was amazing how the gleaming opalescent teeth caused no damage to the soft flesh of the lip. Tca'sk noted another human approaching – Wilma he thought her name was – but neither she nor Damian had lifted their directional eyes to note the other's presence. Tca'sk assumed they would not greet each other and returned the majority of his attention to the conversation.

"I think it is safe to say that," Tca'sk began, but just as Wilma passed Damian, she raised a fist.

"Yo," Damian said, freeing one hand from the datapad he held to slam his own fist into Wilma's.

"Hey," Wilma replied.

The shock surged up Damian's arm and jarred Tca'sk's body. He gripped Damian's shirt, barely remembering to not grip his claws into the soft mammalian skin beneath. Both humans continued walking without breaking their odd two-beat stride and without once raising their eyes to each other. Tca'sk flicked his attention back and forth between them in shock.

That couldn't have been a display of anger or any other passion. Damian's pulse, so clearly visible on the flesh of the neck beside Tca'sk, hadn't even changed its pace. How each human had even been aware of each other in the noisy passageway was a mystery. Their binocular vision was notoriously narrow.

"Tca'sk!" Damian called out, waving his hand for attention. "What do you think?"

"What was that?" Tca'sk demanded.

"I said," Damian replied, "so do you want to go to the deep forest with me?"

"No! I mean yes," Tca'sk began. "I would love to go to the forest, but what was that?" Tca'sk waved in the direction of Wilma's departing back.

"That?" Damian asked with a frown, slowing to a stop.

"Your fists!" Tca'sk clarified, mimicking the action with his two primary manipulators.

"The fist bump?" Damian asked, ruckling his eyebrows.

"Of course you have a name for it," Tca'sk said, slumping down onto Damian's shoulder.

"That? Just a greeting," Damian said with a shrug. "You know, for folks you're cool with."

Tca'sk pondered the complex calculations necessary to near instantly react to the raised fist of a friend glimpsed out of the humans' narrow vision, the minutely controlled force required to not injure the other human, and the concentration needed to maintain their bipedal stride at the same time. He walked over to where the pulsing veins radiated mammalian bioheat from Damian's neck and pressed his primary eyes into the comforting warmth to dim the overstimulation.

"You okay, Tca'sk?" Damian asked in concern.

"Oh, I'm quite fine," Tca'sk said, waving one leg dismissively. "Yes, yes, the deep forest sounds wonderful... just you, me, and no other humans."

"Okay," Damian said slowly.

"Fist bump," Tca'sk chittered. "How many of your greetings involve simulated assault?"

Damian chuckled but seemed to consider the question rhetorical; he shrugged and slipped the datapad under his arm before setting off, whistling.

Humans are Weird – Snow Play

"So it turns out that while I was gone, my kid sister saved up her money from sitting and bought me this sweet snowboard," Human Friend Jameson said, his voice full of eagerness.

Human Friend Jameson was leaning over the cafeteria table eagerly, seemingly heedless of the food on his tray as he gestured at his friend with his fork. The other human seemed completely nonplused by this despite the seven inches of carbon-infused steel being quite capable of being a deadly weapon in the hands of Jameson. Indeed, Kixxitac'll had once seen his friend slay a decently sized predator with a similar implement.

Kixxitac'll shifted the six limbs he was currently ambulating on in the direction of Jameson and his audience. A tray identical to the ones in front of the humans was suspended lightly between his two foremost legs, and on it was balanced his usual liquid nutrients along with a packet of the human delicacy known as flavored gelatin. The cafeteria had produced a new flavor today, and Kizzitac'll was eager to try it. What better conditions than with Human Friend Jameson who also had selected a (much larger) portion of the food?

"Hey, Kixx, have a seat," Jameson greeted him before resuming his presentation to his friends.

"Thank you, Human Friend Jameson," Kixxitac'll replied as he set his tray to the left of Jameson's, giving the human maneuvering room.

"Anyway," Jameson continued, "she wants to take me out on Mount Bachelor as soon as I am out of quarantine, and Mom says that I should bring friends. Any takers?"

There was the usual chorus of disappointed refusals. Most of which seemed to center on the fact that the majority of the marines around him also had plans with their families during that time frame. Two however assured Jameson that they were eager to accompany him on his excursion, and they confirmed dates and times of meeting. A few dispersed, and Kixxitac'll finished his nutrients.

"Human Friend Jameson," he greeted his companion, who was now eagerly spooning the gelatin into his mouth, "do you find the new flavor pleasant?"

"It's okay," Jameson said, dipping his shoulders in a way that indicated either a lack of knowledge or strong emotion. "One kind is pretty much like another."

"I would have to disagree," Kixxitac'll objected. "I much prefer the blue flavor."

"Well, maybe you can get some on leave," Jameson offered.

"Perhaps," Kixxitac'll considered his next words carefully. "Do they have such things at this Mount Bachelor place you spoke of?"

"I think so," Jameson said. "Why do you ask? – Oh."

Kixxitac'll prided himself on his ability to read the incredibly flexible human face and noted precisely when Jameson divined his meaning. "Do you not wish me to come?" Kixxitac'll asked. "Please remember we have pledged honesty to each other."

"No, no," Jameson hurriedly assured him. "I would love for you to come. It is just that the facilities are not set up for you yet, and the climate is fairly extreme."

Kixxitac'll tilted his body to the side curiously, and Jameson activated the wrist-mounted holoprojector all of the humans wore. The skin on his wrist lit up first of a blindingly reflective surface that made Kixxitac'll flinch back and then switched to a rather cozy-looking interior that indeed was fitted for the massive bodies of humans and not for his own smaller frame.

"What is the climate?" he asked, shuddering at the image of the white crystal ground cover.

"Well, here is this week's weather data," Jameson said, scrolling through a few more pages.

Kixxitac'll stared blankly at the display for a moment before turning fully to Jameson's face. "There must be some mistake in that data," Kixxitac'll said firmly. "Otherwise you are telling me you are knowingly exposing your beloved nestmate to prolonged temperatures below the freezing point of water."

Jameson laughed. "She loves it, bud! You should see her pull the halfpipe!"

Humans are Weird – Filter Failure

"And yes," Human Sally said with a gusty mammalian sigh, "I am aware of how bad that sounded."

Twistunder lifted his main gripping appendages in what he had learned humans took to be an interrogative posture. "Then why did you ask the question?" he asked.

"Because I didn't figure out how bad it sounded till after I asked it," Human Sally replied. "I mean in the context... it wasn't so terrible."

"But you did have the context that your coworkers would take it in," Twistunder said, carefully parsing the complex human auditory language. "Are you saying that you were deliberately ignoring data you had access to?"

Human Sally groaned and rolled her eyes. It meant something, but Twistunder was a touch unsure what exactly.

"Look, Twistunder," she said, "sometimes the filter just fails."

"What filter?" Twistunder asked.

"The one between a human's thoughts and her mouth," she explained. "That two decades of learned behavior that we are supposed to have by the time we are legally considered adults."

Twistunder pondered this. Perhaps it was simply one of those mysteries that they would have to accept about their new allies. But still...

"And you truly expressed that you found it odd that people..." Twistunder paused as he worked to repeat the near gibberish phrase the human had used.

"Look," Human Sally interrupted him, "I know how to make stuff work how it really isn't supposed to, right? Jury-rigging, we call it."

"One of humanity's most useful skillsets," Twistunder replied. *And its most terrifying*, he thought privately. Though the thought that a fully adult, non-neuro compromised human couldn't control what they said was perhaps a close second.

"So in that context my statement made sense," Human Sally said, nodding her head. "If I know a different way to do something with the tools at hand, I don't see why it would disturb someone I am benefiting by doing that."

"Perhaps you should state it that way in the future," Twistunder suggested.

"I suppose you're right," Human Sally replied.

"For the record, please state the phrase you used earlier," Twistunder requested.

"I just don't understand why folks get so uncomfortable when I offer to misuse knives."

Humans are Weird – Smiley Faces

"Quartermaster?" Fifty-seven Clicks approached the Undulate cautiously, staying safely above his gripping range and circling slowly.

It wasn't like there was active hostility between their species, not like the hostility that burned low and fierce between the winged kin and those earth crawlers. No, one had to be careful with Undulates because it was just so easy to miss each other. Fifty-seven Clicks's small body and his quick-flitting motion made him as hard for the quartermaster to perceive as it was for the winged kin to see the slow-moving lump against the floor.

"Ah, Fifty-seven Clicks," the quartermaster said as he raised several sensory-rich appendages to find Fifty-seven Clicks in the air.

"I have a request," Fifty-seven Clicks stated quickly. "I would like to be assigned the lighter mobile vices. I would like to exchange all of my current supply for the new type if possible, but even one would be a benefit to my work."

The quartermaster was quiet for a long period, but his raised appendages waved gently in the air. Fifty-seven Clicks shifted in agitation as he waited for the slower Undulate to process his request.

"Forgive me," the Undulate said when he finally dropped his appendages. "I am unaware of any difference in the mobile vices save for the standard size variation."

"The ones that come in multiple color schemes and have a significant portion of the flat gripping surface removed for weight concerns," Fifty-seven Clicks explained.

"What leads you to believe that such a thing is in our stores?" the quartermaster asked. "I have not seen such a thing."

"Human Smith had several in the common room today," Fifty-seven Clicks replied.

The Undulate expanded out his appendages and then relaxed them in a gesture that translated to a sigh of very well. "Of course it was a human," the quartermaster said glumly. "I can assure you no such item came through our base supplies—"

"Human Smith must have ordered it personally," Fifty-seven Clicks said in sudden understanding. He gave a disgruntled chirp and landed on a high shelf.

"Perhaps if you bring me an example of the item in question, I can order some for a feasibility study?" the quartermaster suggested.

Fifty-seven Clicks took off again in delight. That was the thing about having Undulates around. They were so good at figuring out ways around things. He darted back across the base and begged to borrow one of the mobile vices from Human Smith. Smith handed it over easily enough, admonishing him to bring it back. Fifty-seven Clicks flew the bright red folded metal back to the quartermaster.

"This!" he called out, holding up the vice.

The quartermaster took it in his gripping appendages and twisted it this way and that, humming thoughtfully. "I do not know that I could justify this," he finally said. "These three cuts sacrifice quite a bit of strength, and the weight saved is negligible."

"Maybe negligible to a land crawler!" Fifty-seven Clicks snapped. "Every gram counts when you have to carry everything with you on your wings!"

"Could you get the initial justification from the human?" the Undulate asked. "Surely they did a feasibility study before altering their design."

"Humans made these things?" Fifty-seven Clicks asked in surprise. "I thought we did."

"No," the Undulate waved a gripping appendage in dismissal. "The humans developed these to hold their documents together. Their actual designation is 'binder paper clips.'"

"Very well," Fifty-seven Clicks said. "You just need me to get the formally stated logic for the modifications, correct?"

"Yes, specifically why the metal was punched out in this specific pattern," the Undulate said, waving the vice to display the three holes in the metal. "I cannot determine what structural purpose it serves."

Fifty-seven Clicks sped out and returned far more slowly, radiating so much annoyance and befuddled irritation that even the quartermaster noticed it.

"Were you not successful?" he asked.

"Humans," Fifty-seven Clicks muttered as he landed on the shelf.

"Did Smith not have access to the justifications?" the quartermaster asked.

"No," Fifty-seven Clicks said curtly.

"Did he know the justifications?" the quartermaster prompted. "Even a colloquial understanding might give me enough to get a study justified."

"Oh, he knew," Fifty-seven Clicks said with a sigh.

The quartermaster poised his gripping appendage expectantly.

"The three-hole pattern," Fifty-seven Clicks explained, "is a 'smiley face,' and the justification is that it was 'cute.'"

A long moment stretched between them.

"Humans," the quartermaster muttered.

"Humans," Fifty-seven Clicks agreed.

"Well, I will try," the quartermaster offered. "But I advise you now… not since the Klath Beast incident has any feasibility study been justified because of human-perceived cuteness."

"Thanks anyway," Fifty-seven Clicks said glumly as he flew off. Maybe he could trade for one of Smith's.

Humans are Weird – A Little Thing

"You seem particularly cheerful, Ranger Dodge," Twistunder commented as the human strode up to the jeep.

"That I am, Twist, buddy. That I am," Survey Core Ranger Mack Dodge confirmed as his long, jointed limb lifted with a terrifying ease to toss his backpack into the vehicle.

Twistunder rotated his body, appendages spread out as far as they could go in what humans called his 'wet mop phase.' The last, lingering rays of sunlight turned his skin a dark amber that seemed to meld into the green of the jeep's hood. Mack was taking his time to organize their tools in the cargo area, so Twistunder felt comfortable lingering in the sunlight.

"What has pleased you so much?" Twistunder asked after a moment.

Mack hummed over the netting he was securing over the gear. "Well," Mack finally said, "you know that the inspector is here?"

"Oh, yes!" Twistunder replied as he inched across the hood, following the sunlight. "Did you interact with him?"

"Yep," Mack replied. "He swung by in one of those flyers, the insulated little bio-dome ones."

Twistunder could have laughed derisively if he had felt like sharing his contempt of the soft-appendaged bureaucrat with his friend, but as close as he and Ranger Dodge were, one didn't flush your fetid algae around friends. So Twistunder only gave an interrogative hum.

"Anyway," Mack continued as the last beams began to slip off the side of the jeep, and Twistunder gave up on his bathing. "He was watching me hammer in the probe spikes and complimented me on my handiness."

Twistunder climbed over the windshield and dropped down into the driver's seat. He secured the protective restraint around him, secured the steering wheel with his primary gripping appendages, and held out his secondary appendages expectantly.

"Nice try, Twist," Mack said as he opened the driver's door. "Move it."

Twistunder gripped the buckle of the restraints, and a brief scuffle ensued. Mack first tried to simply lift him out of the seat by force, and Twistunder couldn't resist humming in amusement when Mack gave a grunt of frustration. Humans might be able to drive ten-centimeter-long spikes into solid rock, but no species beat an Undulate for gripping power when they didn't want to give up their place.

"Come on, Twist," Mack demanded. "We've been over this. I am not letting you drive."

"I passed the test," Twistunder said in his most logical tone. "I am certified."

"You passed the written test," Mack snapped. "Your species is not meant to hurtle along at driving speeds."

"And yours is?" Twistunder asked. He lifted one gripping appendage to tap the controls. "Correct me if I am wrong, but this speed indicator goes much higher than –what is your maximum running speed again?"

"Faster than yours!" Mack said.

He gave up pulling and flattened his hand against the seat back, sliding it down until he gripped the base of the restraint. Twistunder divined his plan and decided that cheating was in order. He freed about a quarter of his appendages from the seat, at which Mack gave a cry of triumph, and dug them into the human's ribcage and wiggled. Mack howled in frustration but somehow continued to wedge Twistunder off the seat.

"You are developing your resistance to tickling," Twistunder observed as Mack shoved him over into the passenger seat.

"Not that I have much choice in the matter," Mack muttered as they fought one final tugging war over the seatbelt. "You little bugger."

"I do wish to develop this skill," Twistunder pointed out as he finally buckled himself into the passenger seat. "And your charter does call for exchanging information freely."

"It also calls for not getting people killed," Mack replied as he started the engine.

"It can't be more complex than flying a glider," Twistunder pointed out.

"They have a max speed of what," Mack asked, "ten or fifteen?"

"So the inspector complimented you?" Twistunder asked.

Mack shot him a sideways glance at the change in topic but continued driving. "My handiness," Mack said, and a proud smile replaced his irritated look.

Twistunder folded his appendages under himself thoughtfully. "You refer of course to the fact that you are almost as proficient in tasks with both sides of your appendages?"

"Yup," Mack replied, grinning wide enough to show his teeth now.

"You are a decorated Survey Core Ranger, Friend Mack Dodge," Twistunder said carefully.

"Yeah?" Mack replied.

"That means you have achieved honor in the disciplines of both body and mind at the highest level," Twistunder went on, proud to remember the humans separated the two. Such a strange concept.

"And so?" Mack asked.

"Why are you so pleased over recognition that your appendages all function properly?" Twistunder asked. "And why did the inspector think to compliment that?"

"It might be a little thing," Mack said with a shrug. "But I worked hard to bring Lefty up to par, and I'm proud of it. Why wouldn't he compliment it?"

"Did you injure your left appendages seriously?" Twistunder asked, raising a few sensory-rich appendages to examine his friend.

"What?" Mack frowned. "No I – oh right, you guys don't go in for bi-lateral symmetry, so you don't get bi-lateral asymmetry. No, it's unusual for humans to be able to use both hands equally. We have a dominant hand and a non-dominant hand."

"Ah," Twistunder replied. "That is interesting. I suppose the inspector was briefed on this and was showing off his knowledge of human anatomy."

"Could be," Mack replied.

"Another question?" Twistunder asked.

"Shoot, bud," Mack said.

"Do you name all of your appendages?" Twistunder asked.

Uproarious laughter was his only reply.

Humans are Weird – Candles

When Forty-five Trills flew into the base security office, he was not expecting to see the current security officer pointedly ignoring a fire alarm.

"Officer Seventy-seven Clicks?" Forty-five Trills demanded. "There is a fire in the human's compartment of the base."

"I am aware," the officer waved the statement away with a flick of his wing without lifting his eyes from a readout of the exterior fences.

"Well?" Forty-five Trills demanded.

The officer nudged a datapad with his wing claw and returned to his perusal of the readouts. Forty-five Trills picked up the datapad and activated it. The text scrolled slowly across the screen:

It is a candle.

The human in the room is using it to 'meditate.'

Staring at the flame is supposed to help the human 'clear her mind.'

It will not affect the oxygen balance in the base.

I have gotten the human to sign a document saying she will not leave the open flame unattended.

If any further action is required, some other deluded sap can waste their breath arguing with the human.

Forty-five Trills wrinkled his brows in irritation. He had been warned that prolonged exposure to humans was detrimental to protocol, but this was his first personal experience with it. He sighed and shifted his wings on his back. The 'candle' flame wasn't really a threat, but it was so unnecessary. Forty-five Trills weighed the trouble of confronting the human against the danger of setting the precedent of letting candles burn.

"You really don't want to," Seventy-seven Clicks said, seeming to sound his depth without even looking at him.

Forty-five Trills sighed again. He was probably right.

Humans are Weird – Enough C4

"And Commander Grimes agreed with my analysis, sir," the young human was explaining.

Commandant Twirls idly wondered, not for the first time, why the human was forcing himself into that rigid death-like posture while giving his report. All the humans who came before him did it. He wondered if he was curious enough about it to look up the reason in the human behavioral archives. He realized the human had ceased talking, leaving only the soft pulsing of the great central fluid and gaseous pumps of the mammal to fill the room with ambient sound. Deciding that the human wished a response, the Commandant raised his primary gripping appendages in what he hoped mimicked the human's placating body language. He did not want to frighten the young Ranger.

"So to summarize," Commandant Twirls began, "you observed the rapidly reproducing species that had infested the ship and determined through practical experimentation that the infestation could not be eliminated or controlled."

The human bobbed his cranial mass once quickly to confirm the statement. His skin flushed with a rainbow of colors. The spectrum indicated sick horror and shame if the Commandant was any judge of human character. The great pumps began to work faster and then fell out of unison as the human used the gaseous pumps to maintain control over the fluid one. The Commandant would have liked to attempt to soothe the human, but he was afraid to condescend to the youngster, so he continued but added a reminder to his summary.

"You are not being chastised for your choices, Ranger," Commandant Twirls assured him. "The species was identified, and it was a non-sentient replicant threat. The Central University confirms the field assessment you performed. Now, you evacuated the lower section of your survey ship and detonated the entire ship's supply of the human explosive designated C-4 in the affected section."

"Plus the stuff we were carrying out to Gamma base," the human added.

Twirls noted with relief that the human was displaying less stress, and some colors of pleasure even played across the stripes on his face. Though the concept that remembering a giant, near fatal explosion was the cause of this pleasure was disturbing.

"Indeed. You detonated the supply and destroyed the central reproductive chamber of the infestation. This further exposed the interior of that section of the ship to open space."

"Yes, sir," the human replied.

"Here is the one question the council has," Twirls began gently. "And do recall that we are not going to ultimately override the decisions of our field agents in such a situation. You did preserve all the lives of your crew and protected the local inhabited sector. However, we do want to understand the logic of the next step."

"I understand," the human stated.

"For the record then," Commandant Twirls said, "your own analysis shows that you believed the threat had been eliminated by the use of the C-4. Why then did you jettison the infected portions of the ship and take the next steps recorded in the log?"

"We didn't think the C-4 was enough, sir," the human replied. "I mean there was always a chance one of the sub-queens had laid an egg-cyst in a hard-to-reach place, and we decided that the risk of one of those hatching halfway home wasn't worth the reward of having the added stability of the lower superstructure and supplies that were left after the detonation."

"So you jettisoned that segment of the ship," the Commandant concluded, running his trained reading appendages over the report he was lying on, "sent it on a collision course with an asteroid, then voided the contents of your backup power supply, causing a nuclear detonation when the supply collided with the asteroid and the jettisoned section."

The human's face blanched so deeply that the pulsing blood vessel network was visible under the stripes.

"It was the only way to be sure," he muttered.

Humans are Weird – Aposematism

"And then the human picked me up and said no in that particular way," Idlyspins said, tightening his tertiary appendages in furious exasperation. "The way that means there is no point in arguing."

"How rude," Halftwist replied. "One might almost suspect that we have been collectively conditioning humans to pick us up to cuddle at the slightest provocation or sign of danger."

"It wasn't about that," Idlyspins insisted, tossing his gripping appendages up in frustration. "It wasn't at all uncomfortable. The point is I wanted that sample. I am a zoologist. That was a zoo!"

"Well, the humans have certainly affected your grammar," Halftwist replied, letting half his appendages droop in amusement. "I must say… it is rather impressive that you can convert sloppy human habits from sound to motion."

"Again, that is not the point!" Idlyspins insisted. "The human just picked me up and carried me away."

"From the danger," Halftwist pointed out.

"From an invisible danger that only he could sound!" Idlyspins growled in frustration. "From a zoo that was a thousandth of my mass, let alone his."

"From the report, it sounded like a reasonable assessment," Halftwist observed. "A venomous invertebrate is nothing to mess with given how thin our outer membrane is."

"There was no evidence of venom!" Idlyspins insisted. "We didn't get nearly close enough for the chemoreceptors to take any readings. The human made that distinction based only on the external colors and patterns. Patterns that I couldn't discern."

"Do remember that the council specifically petitioned for a human crew for this mission," Halftwist said. "Do you know why?"

"Of course!" Idlyspins replied. "This is a class four survival level planet. We needed a predator to protect us."

"And that protection extends to perceiving dangers that we cannot," Halftwist said firmly. "I will not censor the squad mate who was sent out to keep you safe for taking action to keep you safe."

"But I need that sample!" Idlyspins insisted. "Gathering the native flora is the primary reason we came to this planet. There was no reason for us to hire the humans to protect us if they prevent us from doing our jobs through that protection!"

"Understood," Halftwist said. "Fortunately the humans have provided a solution to this particular issue."

"Really?" Idlyspins asked cautiously. "Does this so-called solution involve sticking a human in a preposterous battle suit and me getting shoved in a glorified hauling sack with a sad excuse for an appendage extender on it?"

Halftwist curled up his appendages in amusement and began tapping on the screen in front of him. "Yes, you were with the *Scorpion* crew, weren't you?" he asked.

"It was supposed to be a scientific expedition," Idlyspins muttered. "The only data we ended up gathering was on the physiological effects of extended periods of terror on scientists."

"No, no," Halftwist told him as the printer began to hum. "This is a remote device. You place it in the suspected environment and passively collect the fauna. The human can drop it off and pick it up while in a defensive armor."

"Wouldn't that be subject to degradation?" Idlyspins asked, stiffening his appendages in suspicion.

"Well, they don't use it underwater," Halftwist replied. "Be warned. Don't touch the center of the folding area. We had to ship the last tech who did that off to the medical facility on Globual."

Idlyspins looked at the flat printout with interest and mentally folded it into functionality. He cooed softly in surprise. The third-dimensional triangle should be a very effective trap for the invertebrates he was studying. The adhesive center really needed no warning. What sort of idiot would touch that?

"There will be plentiful incidental traps," Idlyspins muttered as he folded the device into shape.

"That is your issue," Halftwist said, waving his gripping appendages dismissively. "And I don't see how having more samples is a bad thing. Does this solve your problem?"

"Not the problem of overprotective humans," Idlyspins pointed out as he lifted the now complete trap.

"I am sorry," Halftwist said, dropping his appendages in irritation. "But we have a legal policy against discouraging friendly interactions with a species of predators that are forty times our mass on average."

Idlyspins grumbled as he left the room.

Idlyspins wasn't grumbling when he returned for more traps several cycles after their conversation.

"I am not sulking!" he muttered when Halftwist couldn't quite keep the smug pose out of his appendages.

"The human was right," Halftwist said cheerfully.

"He was only able to identify the venom and poison level of the samples with eighty percent accuracy," Idlyspins returned. "It is not a fail proof system."

"Only eighty percent," Halftwist observed. "Practically

useless."

"I might be adopting bad human grammar," Idlyspins growled, "but you are adopting horrible human sarcasm."

Humans are Weird – Jump

"Friend Forty-seven Clicks!" Twistunder greeted the Winged who was hunched over the communal pool. "It is good to see you!"

"Ah?" the Winged raised his amber head and blinked as he focused his attention on the Undulate. "It is good to see you too, Friend Twistunder."

Twistunder swam leisurely up to the prominence where Forty-seven Clicks was staring over the surface of the pool. Twistunder felt a stirring of unease as he approached. He was not particularly good at reading the emotions of the flying mammals. However, the relative increase in folds and creases in Forty-seven Clicks's facial membrane would seem to indicate distress.

"Do you wish to talk about your emotions, Friend Forty-seven Clicks?" Twistunder asked.

Forty-seven Clicks bared his teeth and squinted his eyes in a gesture that even Twistunder could see was frustration. "I would rather talk about human madness," Forty-seven Clicks chirped out in anger.

"What did a human do this time?" Twistunder asked, genuinely curious.

"Not a human," Forty-seven Clicks corrected as he dipped the tip of his wing in the water. "The humans' psychology as a whole."

"How so?" Twistunder asked.

"I was out on a long-range scouting run," Forty-seven Clicks said with a sigh, slumping down onto the perch. "We had a transport, but it was flatland only, so we had to get out and fly or climb to explore."

"There was a human in your flight?" Twistunder asked.

"Yes, a healthy, young one," Forty-seven Clicks replied. "So the expedition is going just fine, but we get to a steep cliff where we needed to get out of the transport. I flew up. I needed to rest at least five times, and even the human needed to rest from his climbing, but eventually we reached the crest. The winds were strong, so I followed protocol and attached myself to the human's neck harness. After we finished the formal survey, the human walked to the edge of the cliff and just… stared."

"What was he staring at?" Twistunder asked.

"The emptiness of space," Forty-seven Clicks replied. "That is all we can see at that distance even with our superior sight."

"Then what happened?" Twistunder pressed.

"The human's heart rate accelerated," Forty-seven Clicks said. "His breathing increased. Something was stimulating him."

"But all he was looking at was the emptiness of space?" Twistunder asked.

"Then he asked me… without making eye contact… if I ever got the urge to jump off of cliffs too," Forty-seven Clicks said.

Twistunder pondered this a moment. "That phrasing would imply that the human had the urge to jump off of the cliff."

"Yes!" Forty-seven Clicks hissed out.

"Humans cannot fly," Twistunder continued.

"Of course not with those ridiculously giant bodies!" Forty-seven Clicks said.

"It would be fatal to leap from the height you describe," Twistunder said with rising horror.

"So I called off the mission and reported the human to the psychologist!" Forty-seven Clicks explained.

"That seems perfectly reasonable," Twistunder said.

Forty-seven Clicks threw himself down on the perch and hung his head over the water. "You would think," Forty-seven Clicks said. "But apparently it was simply my ignorance that interfered with the mission. The urge to jump from fatal heights is a psychological standard in humans that I would have known about had I read the informational packet fully."

Silence settled over the friends, and Twistunder mused over this revelation. "Having impulses that you do not act on is one of the defining elements of sapience," Twistunder said slowly. "But I have never heard of such an illogical example of this."

"Well, now you have," Forty-seven Clicks said with a sigh.

Humans are Weird – New Position

"But if the title simply means assistant morale officer—"

"With denotations of alien life forms," Flipoff interjected.

Twistaround rotated his support appendages in irritation, sending a rippling shrug along his core. He debated telling the arrogant officer what his name really translated to in the human dialects and like every other time decided against it. He shifted the datapad in his gripping appendages and continued speaking.

"If that is the direct translation," he said, "even with all associated denotations, I don't see the need to create a new named position. Just inform the crews that there needs to be two morale officers on any ship with a human or two, a master and a student."

"Because," Flipoff sent a wave of his appendages up in a signal that one usually used with fresh budlings who were asking too many questions about the color of algae fields, "this is not a learning position. The goal is for the new officer to know more about humans… at least in this one field than the chief morale officer."

Twistaround tightened his appendages in stubborn perplexity. "And you expect me to be an expert on this state of mind?" he demanded, feeling a little proud of knowing the last noun. Centralized nervous systems were so very fascinating.

"No," Flipoff replied with a grim flick of an appendage. "You are simply an officer with more than a month of experience with human crews like all the others we contacted. We expect you to become the expert."

"I have only been trained in observational psychology," Twistaround observed uneasily. "I would hardly be prepared to react

"Good!" interrupted Flipoff. "Acting on your observations will fall to the morale officer. It is best you understand that going in."

Twistaround fought down the offense that inspired in him. It was one thing when one of the fast land species interrupted a flowing conversation. It was quite another when an Undulate who *knew better* did it. Yes, there was more than a little cosmic irony in Flipoff's name. Either that or he understood the connotations and chose his translation deliberately. However, Twistaround did not sense that much of a sense of humor in the abrupt officer.

"So my job," Twistaround began as he examined the description yet again, trying to gain relevant information from the many, many words, "is to observe the human populations, be it one or many, and report to the morale officer for correction of any instance… or chance of… a state of mind that is really not known to exist in our people except as a rare and usually fatal neurological condition… but that humans consider perfectly normal."

"Correct," Flipoff replied. "And to simplify the circumstance, we are naming it with human sounds and written denotation precisely because it rarely affects other species either."

"We are talking about a state of being where the human is suffering from a lack of sufficient threats," Twistaround offered, certain that he had misconstrued the Trisk field report. The small skittering land aliens were perhaps the most like them in appearance despite being an aiming species, but their different life goals made their writing especially hard to decipher.

"Indeed," Flipoff confirmed with no modifiers.

Twistaround expanded his appendages to patiently wait for Flipoff to expand on this, but no such clarification of how Twistaround had misunderstood the concept came. As mad as it sounded, this was his new calling. "I suppose," he said, uncertain of what was expected of him, "that it is very kind of the home pools to expend this many resources to secure the mental health of our new friends."

"There is absolutely nothing altruistic about this move," Flipoff said, assuming a grim pose. "This is strictly for the safety of our crews who have to deal with humans."

"Why must you be so dramatic?" Twistaround finally burst out, exasperated with the posturing of his superior. "What is the worst thing that could possibly happen if a highly skilled and highly trained human gets '*borea*'?"

Humans are Weird – Imaginary Lines

"I heard you had a long and heated talk with the human cartographer," Thirty-two Trills observed as his second-in-command fluttered down onto the branch he was hanging from.

"You could call it that," Three Clicks said with an expressive sigh as he settled down beside his commander.

"Did you write it up?" Thirty-two Trills asked. "It sounded land graph related."

"I took many notes," Three Clicks said, running his winghooks over his sensory horns in an absent grooming gesture. "I do plan to make a full report."

"Well, do… and don't drag me into it," Thirty-two Trills ordered him. "I have quite enough human madness to deal with in my own duties."

However, from the way Three Clicks's fur bushed out and relaxed, he did want to talk about the issue. Thirty-two Trills was estimating the value of his tablet mentally, debating if he couldn't risk dropping it and making a mad dash for freedom before his second-in-command gathered his wits.

"He argued that planetary equators are imaginary," Three Clicks finally burst out.

Thirty-two Trills fluffed out his fur in shock and turned his eyes on Three Clicks. "But I know they use that concept daily!" Thirty-two Trills exclaimed. Then immediately regretted it. *Not his job. Not his job.*

"They do!" Three Clicks answered, gesturing dramatically

with his wings. "They have the equator on their own world and a range of degree lines as well. They simply insist that the equator is, and I quote, 'an imaginary line.' A thing any child of any sentient species can see! A thing understood genetically by countless non-sentient species."

"So," Thirty-two Trills said slowly, "a thing that they use for scientific measurement and suborbital navigation on a daily basis, a thing that is clearly recognized on every spherical world, they consider to be imaginary."

"Yes!" Three Clicks exclaimed. He spread his wings in frustration. "And you should have heard the argument he used. Things about having crossed the equator on a dozen worlds and never having seen one—"

However, the added time allowed the commander to neatly tuck his tablet into his chest pack, and he sprang off the branch, clicking a jaunty tune.

"I'll see it all in your report!" he called out cheerfully.

It really wasn't his problem.

Humans are Weird – Lava

"So the commander of the central flight wants to make a formal ceremony of the act of gratitude," Forty-five Clicks informed the human who was busily strapping something onto his legs. "He—"

Forty-five Clicks stopped speaking as he realized exactly what the human had been trying on. Just to make sure, he flew up to the top of the backpack the human was loading and chirped in, sounding the fragrant depths.

"Why are you packing up this personal heat shielding?" Forty-five Clicks demanded. He wasn't sure why all the fur on his body stood on end, but by the gum of the mother tree, he had learned to trust that instinct.

"I need it to get the samples," the human replied cheerfully.

Forty-five Clicks wasn't one to perch on ceremony even by the loose standards of his people. He leapt up, threw all of his forty grams of mass in the face of the human, and dug his winghooks into the soft flesh under the human's ears. This let him glare furiously into one of the cavernous pupils of the larger mammal.

"What... samples?" Forty-five Clicks demanded.

"Of the lava," the human said quickly. "Hey, winghooks, man."

"Why?" Forty-five Clicks pressed.

"For fun," the human replied.

"Where are you going to get lava from?" Forty-five Clicks demanded as slowly as he could.

"That volcano that just popped," the human replied, gesturing in what Forty-five Clicks assumed was meant to be the direction of the former mountain. It wasn't. How did they survive in nature on their own, the poor directionless things?

"The volcano," Forty-five Clicks said. "The one that nearly killed three flights. The one that took down not only our silverwing atmospheric flyers but also one of your near indestructible helicopters. The one that utterly destroyed hectares of land. The one that is currently spewing ash, gas, and liquid magma."

"It isn't magma after it gets to the surface!" the human insisted.

Forty-five Clicks groaned and loosed the human. He slid down the human's chest until he was caught in the broad hand. The hand that was covered in scars so thick any one of them would have utterly incapacitated his wings and a fresh cut that he knew the human had gained in the rescue operation. Forty-five Clicks sighed and rubbed his eyes.

"You are not going to collect magma—"

"Lava," the human corrected hopefully.

"Lava samples from the volcano," Forty-five Clicks said as firmly as he could. "For fun."

"And why not?" demanded the human.

"I just can't right now," Forty-five Clicks said. "Just go ask the commander."

"Will do then," the human said cheerfully as he set off.

Forty-five Clicks flew up and passed over the backpack once again. He glared at the thermal armor. He had assumed it was only for rescue missions. His mistake.

Humans are Weird – What Rock

"Did you file the samples you collected?" Fourth Sister asked as the human walked past.

The human paused in her movements and frowned in a way that was supposed to indicate thought. "What samples?" she asked.

Fourth Sister clicked her mandibles in confusion and raised her head frill a touch. "You were out on the river's edge collecting mineral samples for the majority of the morning," Fourth Sister said, waving her pale green hands in the direction of the door. "You must have at least eighty kilos of sample material in your quarters."

"Eighty?" the human frowned, and then her face relaxed. "Oh, you mean the rocks."

"Yes," Fourth Sister said with a sigh, letting her frill drop back to lay along her neck. "The 'rocks.' Please remember to label and report them correctly."

"Yeah, no," the human shook her head. "I wasn't collecting those for samples for the base. It was a private thing."

"Oh," Fourth Sister said, pausing the movement of her fingers over the datapad and waiting for the human to continue. However, the human merely shrugged and moved away. Fourth Sister watched her disappear down the corridor with confusion. She considered pursuing the matter, but her datapad chimed to remind her of her next task, and she made a note to bring up the matter again at the midday meal.

She easily found the correct human again at meal time. This human wore a rather large array of outer-ear ornaments. Fourth Sister was quite proud of herself for not flinching back in natural horror from the visual of cold steel piercing not only the outer protective membrane but also the cartilaginous substructure. It was still hard not to think about it as she carefully folded her legs around the human-formed bench.

"Greetings, Human," Fourth Sister said.

The human looked up from her meal, and one of the hairy, protective eye ridges rose, seemingly disconnected from any other movements on her face. Fourth Sister fought down a shudder of revulsion and made a note to research what the gesture meant.

"Susan," the human said.

"Excuse me?" Fourth Sister asked.

"My name," the human said clearly. "What I wish to be called is Susan."

"I see," Fourth Sister said. "Susan. So about our earlier conversation—"

"What earlier conversation?" the human Susan interrupted.

"The one where you informed me that the rocks you collected were not scientific specimens," Fourth Sister clarified.

"What about it?" Susan demanded.

"If they were not specimens, then what were they?" Fourth Sister asked.

"What business is that of yours?" Susan asked, her voice dropping into aggressive tones.

"It is my business to catalog all scientific specimens that are collected by the base population," Fourth Sister explained. "The Ranger Corps requires a designated specimen monitor."

"They didn't have one on Rough End Base," Susan observed.

"It only applies to bases that are near a population center," Fourth Sister explained. "It is to prevent accidental contamination."

"Oh, makes sense," Susan said with a nod. "Well, I was just collecting some rocks for a private merchant project. I checked all the regulations, and the local rivers are all clear for the locals to interact with."

"A merchant project," Fourth Sister repeated as she entered the data in her pad. "You are correct... there is no need for me to report that."

"Good, so we done here?" Susan asked.

"Formally. Yes," Fourth Sister answered. "However," her frill raised in curiosity, "what value do these rocks possess?"

"Oh, nothing intrinsic," Susan said, her face curving into a grin. "I am making pet rocks for the tourists."

"Pet rocks?" Fourth Sister asked.

"Yeah," Susan stooped and dug into a bag by her side. "I bought some printer time and printed out paper boxes and bedding and hand wrote the instructions on the side. See?"

Fourth Sister bent over the box and tilted her head from side to side to get a good look at it. It was a basic carrying box with 'Alien Pet Rock' printed on the front. On the side were instructions for 'training' and 'care' for the rock. Fourth Sister considered it for a long time and lifted her head slowly away.

"Tourists pay money for this?" she finally asked.

Susan burst out in laughter and tossed the box and its contents back into the bag. "Yeah, the humans who come through the city love this sort of thing," she said. "I am thinking about painting green antennae on it to make it more alien."

"Humans buy rocks of no intrinsic value," Fourth Sister said softly.

"If you package it right, they do," Susan said cheerfully. "Now I have to go get the rest ready to take 'em to my vendor."

Humans are Weird – Surf's Up

"So this is what Human Steve has been saving up his printer time for," Twistunder observed as he ambled over the polymer surface.

"Do you have any idea what it is?" Thirty-five Clicks asked from above.

"No," Twistunder replied as he reached on end and draped his gripping appendages over the pointed tip.

"Then why did you request permission to inspect it?" the Winged asked.

"Human Steve was giggling while he made this," Twistunder explained.

"And what does that have to do with the density of midges over the water?" Thirty-five Clicks asked.

Twistunder mused for a moment before replying. "Oh, yes, you're new," the Undulate said.

Thirty-five Clicks bristled in affront, but as the Undulate simply continued his minute inspection of the human creation, the Winged released the load of irritation and fluttered over to him in curiosity.

"I think it looks like a floating colony pontoon," Thirty-five Clicks offered. "But larger."

"It is very broad for such a function, but on reflection I must agree," consented Twistunder. "And what do you make of these protrusions?" He indicated the three triangular forms that rose out of the blunt end of the thing.

"Stabilizers," Thirty-five Clicks said with confidence. "To reduce rolling. Not all species have no concept of up, you know."

"We have a concept of resisting gravity," Twistunder protested. "It just doesn't mean all that much to us."

"Sure, sure," the Winged landed between the protrusions and experimentally nudged one with a wing claw. "Strong but small in proportion to the rest of the float."

"Indeed," Twistunder said.

"Odd that he printed it just now," Thirty-five Clicks observed. "With that wind coming in from the great water, we certainly can't fly, and even you swimming types have declared the best hunting estuaries unsafe."

"The force of the waves on this world would crush us," Twistunder affirmed. "I doubt even the famous internal skeleton of our human friends could withstand the blows."

"So why now?" Thirty-five Clicks asked with growing uneasiness.

"I was concerned," Twistunder admitted, "but your observation on the inadequate size of the stabilizers offers an unclenching explanation."

"Unclenching?" Thirty-five Clicks asked.

"It relieves my tension," Twistunder replied. "This is no doubt only a component of a larger craft. Human Steve is no doubt building it in sections as he saves up enough to print out all the parts."

"That makes sense," Thirty-five Clicks replied. "Consider me unclenched."

"That is not how that word is used," Twistunder said with some affront.

Thirty-five Clicks was about to reply when the human sound of joy (that was far too similar to an emergency alert klaxon) tore through the base. Human Steve burst into the storage room, his bronze skin gleaming, all several square meters of it. Thirty-five Clicks stared in wide-eared shock at the mass of nearly imperceptibly furred dermis. Human Steve was wearing nothing but a small pair of undergarments as he swept up the float. Twistunder had somehow found the speed to slip off the side before this and seemed less shocked than Thirty-five Clicks as they watched the human disappear out the door with the giant float balanced on his head as if it were nothing.

Twistunder never stopped moving. He prodded the stunned Winged as he shuffled by.

"I will contact the medic," Twistunder said. "You get on the cultural database and find out what in the name of my mother's colony 'Surf's up, little dudes!' means."

Humans are Weird – Fairy Rings

"And why did you bring me up here, Eight Clicks?" Quilx'tch demanded as he peeped his primary eye set over the edge of the sensory array. "Way up here?"

"You have more experience observing humans than I do," said the young Winged who had lured him up here. "I require your observations on an odd behavior pattern."

"Unless they are eating or not eating something, there is not much I can offer," Quilx'tch said as he secured his grip on the surface with all eight of his appendages. "Please stop making the air currents worse!"

"There," Eight Clicks landed beside Quilx'tch and focused his binocular vision on a patch of ground far, far below them.

Quilx'tch took in the scene and tried to note anything different. However, the patch of ground indicated by the Winged was indistinguishable from all the others to the nutritional anthropologist. "I see no humans… and therefore no human behavior to comment on!" Quilx'tch snapped out.

"But you do see the fungal growth?" Eight Clicks asked eagerly.

"What fungal growth?" Quilx'tch demanded, edging away from his mammalian companion.

"Oh, right," Eight Clicks muttered. "You Trisk have poor vision."

"Our vision is perfectly adapted to our preferred habitat," Quilx'tch snapped out. "Our pattern recognition at reasonable distances

—"

"Yes, yes," Eight Clicks rudely cut him off. "There is a fungal growth. That *Hexamartin* species is fruiting, and it formed a surface visible pattern. Here." He projected an image of what Quilx'tch assumed was the ground below. A ring of the fungal fruiting bodies had indeed sprung up.

"Are the humans eating them?" Quilx'tch asked, curious now.

"No, they are poisonous, I think," Eight Clicks said. "But how can I, ah! Like this!" The Winged shifted the projection so that it overlaid the reality that Quilx'tch was seeing below him. The ring was indicated by a cluster of blue dots against the dusky orange of the ground cover. "Now just wait until the shift for lunch ends," Eight Clicks instructed.

Quilx'tch was rather interested now, so he waited as instructed. The tonal alarm sounded for the end of the lunch cycle, and the humans and Shatar spilled out of the communal cafeteria. This was an interesting position to observe mass behavior from, Quilx'tch decided.

"Now keep an eye on the fungal growth," Eight Clicks instructed him.

The mass of bipeds had reached the indicated spot on the ground, and Quilx'tch grew attentive as the pattern became obvious. The more brightly colored Shatar paced across the space without pause. The humans however, even with their lesser mobility, swerved to avoid passing through the circle formed by the fruiting bodies.

"Fascinating," Quilx'tch clicked softly.

"The pattern holds too," Eight Clicks said eagerly. "I have recorded this behavior in over twenty locations."

"Is it conscious?" Quilx'tch asked.

"Sometimes, sometimes not," Eight Clicks said. "When it is conscious, I have noted them indicating body language that the Shatar's lack of avoidance behavior causes the humans distress.

However, the majority of the times it appears to be an instinctive reaction."

"They do eat some fungal fruiting bodies," Quilx'tch observed. "Perhaps it is simply an ingrained nutrient maximization behavior to avoid damaging fungal bodies that provided sustenance?"

"That is a sound theory," Eight Clicks admitted.

"However?" Quilx'tch prompted even as he watched the flow of humans.

"When I brought my observations to Human Friend O'Beirne, he did not wish to answer," Eight Clicks said.

"You must have misunderstood him," Quilx'tch protested. "Friend O'Beirne has almost no social inhibitions. Why… he spent the better part of a day discussing reproduction with me."

"I am aware," Eight Clicks said, flaring his wings in agitation. "That conversation was recorded. But I assure you. He has inhibitions about this. I was able to ascertain that it involved a human superstition."

"A superstition?" Quilx'tch asked eagerly.

There was a vast blank of knowledge on current human superstitions. While that was well outside of his focus, it was still a fascinating topic.

"The only specifics he offered was the term 'ferry circles,'" Eight Clicks continued. "And he seemed terribly embarrassed by the observation. He displayed that odd behavior where he answers the question at inaudible volumes and in a direction away from you."

"Ah," Quilx'tch muttered. "We must proceed carefully."

"Indeed," Eight Clicks agreed. "Why won't humans walk through a ferry circle?"

Humans are Weird – Aurora

"Don't misunderstand me," Twistunder said, carefully articulating each word. He was perched on a rock about the same size as his human friend's head, and the cold was seeping into his gripping appendages. He dearly looked forward to the time when their friendship advanced to the state that he could ask to actually sit on the blessedly warm head. "It is not that I do not find the sky... oh... that was a double negative... I do find... is a double positive better?"

The Undulate sensed that his human companion was giving him a disapproving glare. At least Twistunder thought Bryant was glaring at him. Bryant's facial positioning clearly indicated displeasure, but it was always hard to tell which direction a human's bipedal form was indicating. Twistunder considered his options and remembered that they were off duty.

"My apologies," Twistunder said, reaching over to pat Bryant's arm with a gripping appendage. "You are resting. I will stop asking questions."

"Questions are fine," Bryant said, leaning back to rest his head on his arm and focusing on the northern sky again. "Just not about grammar."

"Why do you consider that particular part of the sky," Twistunder lifted both of his gripping appendages in what humans called 'air quotes' and his people called intensifiers, "*more* beautiful than any other?"

"The aurora, Twist!" Bryant exclaimed, gesturing toward the north with one hand. "Just look at it. Red, pink, blue, green, all the colors now."

Twistunder focused as hard on his photoreceptors as he could, spreading his motile appendages to catch more of the heavenly light. After a moment, his mass overwhelmed the gripping power of the few appendages he had left gripping the cold, hard rock. He swayed and latched onto the rock again.

"I suppose the unusually organized patterned behavior is somewhat novel," Twistunder admitted. "It is rare to see such large effects other than due to the solar winds."

Bryant frowned thoughtfully and twisted his head over to look at the Undulate again. "So we agree that the sky is beautiful, but you don't think that the aurora looks any more beautiful than the rest of the sky?"

"Indeed," Twistunder said, making sure to shrug the appendages analogous to his shoulders.

"But we see color the same, right?" Bryant asked. "I mean you recognize black, white, and the three main colors."

"Correct," Twistunder replied. "I greatly enjoyed the dot charts your universities shared with us."

"But you think that plain black and white is just as beautiful as all that color?" Bryant asked, waving to the north again.

Twistunder refocused on the night sky in mild confusion. The swirling atmospheric colors, pricked by the many-toned stars, created the usual near infinite color palette – that sense of divine depth that was washed out in the burning light of daystars.

"'The night sky bleeds with every color of the coral,'" Twistunder quoted the old children's poem.

Bryant stared at him, and a shocked look spread across his face, closely followed by a look of giddy expectation. "You see the night sky in all the colors?" he asked.

"And you only see it as black and white," Twistunder replied, realization dawning. "That is why the aurora phenomenon is so valuable to you."

"The xeno-biologists must have missed this somehow," Bryant said with a grin.

"Well, our species did only meet recently," Twistunder replied.

"Hey," Bryant sat up and held out his hands to Twistunder. "Let's get back to the base and write this up. My contract says I get a bonus for new interspecies discoveries." To Twistunder's delight, the moment Bryant's hands closed around him, the human gave an exclamation of displeasure. "You are freezing, Twist. Here... hold onto my head."

Twistunder gripped the shaved surface in delight as they moved back towards the base. This was a fascinating discovery really. If humans were blind to the colors of the night sky, that would cause a stir in several different disciplines, and if the discovery fell to the Undulates, that would greatly increase their prestige at the University. He examined the glowing stripes that covered the back of the human's neck with the photo receptors on his gripping appendages. If their sense of color was so limited, could they even see their own bioluminescence? That might explain the seemingly random distribution of self-depiction pigment in their visual art. He resolved to ask Bryant about it after the human completed his report.

Humans Are Weird – Pronking

"*Yeah, my kids back home do that all the time,*" the human on the screen was saying with a smile. "*The girls do it more than the boys though.*"

"As you can see, the behavior is near universal in the species," the behavioral anthropologist explained as he paused the video. "However, when asked to explain it—" he waved his manipulators to indicate the screen as it resumed playing.

"*Why?*" the human asked as its face wrinkled with that bizarre, fleshy movement that defined all of the endoskeleton species. "*I don't know. It's fun, I guess?*"

"Fun," Quilx'tch said. "The universal catch-answer humans have for all questions beginning in why."

"Indeed," the behavioral anthropologist agreed. "However, I have a working theory that explains it!"

Quilx'tch fought the urge to tighten his legs under him in irritation. Why was he here? He was here to offer social support to his fellow anthropologist. The same he expected to receive when he went on about nutrient levels in chicken soup, so he gamely focused on the graphs and data his coworker displayed.

"You have a theory that explains the human behavior of skipping?" Quilx'tch asked politely.

The behavioral anthropologist clicked eagerly and summoned two more screens. Quilx'tch watched the previous screen of one of the younger soldiers on the base moving across the exercise ground. He was neither walking nor running. Instead he was using every alternating bipedal step to thrust himself up against the pull of the gravity well.

151

"Skipping must require a lot of calories," Quilx'tch observed.

"A massive expenditure," his coworker agreed. "And here is a very similar behavior that the humans recorded in wild and domestic animals."

Quilx'tch ran his primary eyes over the displays. "But those are quadrupeds," Quilx'tch pointed out. "And have completely different diets. They rely on—"

"Yes, yes!" the behavioral anthropologist waved a hand dismissively. "But the differences in structure only serve to display the similarity in behavior!"

Quilx'tch bristled in shock at the abrupt dismissal. The rudeness was – well, it was human, Quilx'tch remembered with a release of tension. His coworker had been among the humans the longest. It was only logical that he had picked up a few of their quirks. Quilx'tch refocused on the screens.

"All three behaviors involve needlessly thrusting up against the central gravity well," Quilx'tch summarized. He gave a short hop to demonstrate.

"Yes!" his coworker enthused. "And the humans have already described and explained the behavior in other species… but!" He held up his primary manipulator. "They have not thought to apply it to themselves!"

Quilx'tch kept his primary eyes on the behavioral anthropologist but snuck a pair of legs under his abdomen to begin lightly tapping on the keyboard he projected there. He found himself once more grateful for learning to divide his attention so well in the academy.

"And then I discovered the age gap!" his coworker went on eagerly. "Human young display the behavior near constantly, but adults only display it when they are alone or when they think there is a minimal chance of being observed by other species!"

Quilx'tch gave an absent click of confirmation as the other went on.

"And then the mass division is quite clear among adult humans. With an inverse correlation between mass and frequency of skipping." The behavioral anthropologist paused and looked eagerly at Quilx'tch, this time waiting the appropriate time for a response.

Quilx'tch stretched a bit and then settled down again. "I am a nutritional anthropologist," he finally said. "I can draw no conclusions from your most excellent research data, my friend."

"It is pronking!" the behavioral anthropologist said with a happy titter. "The humans pronk just as much as the wild quadrupeds."

"So your theory is that humans skip to convince predators that the caloric expenditure of catching them would exceed the caloric gain of eating them?" Quilx'tch asked.

"Indeed!" his coworker said brightly.

"I see," Quilx'tch said, tapping a manipulator against the floor thoughtfully. "That does seem logical."

His coworker took that as encouragement to go on, and Quilx'tch slipped his legs back under his abdomen with a vexed click of his mandibles. He had reports to get done.

Humans are Weird – Cold

Bright points of light burned down out of a cloudless sky. The stars were only faintly obscured by the light of two small moons. Beneath them a small huddle of structures stood stoutly against the spreading frost. Between the starlight reflecting off of the ice and the giant silver satellite dish standing noble guard over the buildings, an artist might have called it beautiful, idyllic even.

The screaming started around whatever the local equivalent of three A.M. was. The human inhabitants of the pseudo-military instillation woke instantly and grabbed for whatever weapons were at hand. The situation was ripe with tension. Which, due to the rapid situational analysis natural selection bred into people with a penchant for survival, almost immediately gave way to irritation, confusion, and the occasional burst of profanity.

"Get it off! Get it off! My back! Cold!"

The frantic screams were first joined by shouts of warning and then rough laughter. A string of profanity-laced comments marched heavily through the cold, dense air. Followed by a shriek.

"I don't care! Get. It. Off!"

There was a stern mumble that from the tone could only have come from a sergeant.

"Okay, okay!"

A faint squealing of discomfort interrupted the proper words.

"Cold! Cold! Get *him* off then!"

There was a bit more indistinguishable murmuring, and as no further disturbance was forthcoming, the weapons were returned to their sheaths, and the camp returned to sleep.

Betty Adams
Memo to All Rough End Base Personnel

Re: Acceptable Behavior in Life-Threatening Situations and Social Duties to Fellow Sapients in Life-Threatening Situations

The command staff asks all personnel to remember that not all species inhabiting Rough End Base have the same tolerance levels for physical contact. Furthermore, some species that indulge in full body organism rest (i.e., sleep), humans specifically, have different rules for acceptable physical contact when in the sleep state than while awake. Please remember that a human in the sleep state is incapable of differentiating between a native predator and a friendly ally. It is suggested that a sleeping human be woken up from no less that {three feet} away by throwing hard objects at them and vocalizing a non-threatening greeting.

The humans of Rough End Base do recognize that the increasingly harsh conditions can be life-threatening to their smaller and less endothermic allies. They are also aware that their large mammalian bodies generate plentiful excess heat. As a rule, they are perfectly willing to offer any aid to their fellow sapients capable of. However, please remember to obtain permission from the selected human before utilizing this benefit of their presence.

A human who is woken from the sleep state by "a gazillion tiny freezing pseudopods crawling up my bare back" is prone to make loud, disruptive noises, attempt to remove the unidentified object from his/her back, and leap wildly around the sleeping space without a care for who or what they might step on. This can lead to the disruption of sleep for others in the sleep state, injuries to both the human and whoever is attached to their back, and significant mental trauma for all participants.

If one finds that one must obtain warmth immediately to sustain one's continued existence and the proper permission cannot be obtained, it is suggested that one holds on tight.

Humans are Weird – A Good Long Walk

"But have you not performed the necessary amount of muscular contraction to maintain your functionality for the day?" Twistunder asked as he scampered after his friend.

Human Friend Mack was briskly striding around the airlock of the base searching for one particular personal radiations shield. "Yeah, I guess," he answered absently. "Are you sure you haven't seen my hat?"

"I have not," Twistunder assured him. "However, Human Friend Rob's radiation shield is there on the peg, and it is the same size."

Human Friend Mack rolled his eyes. "I can't take Rob's hat, Twist," he said. "It's just, ah!" He flushed with triumph as he discovered the radiation shield he had been searching for under a thermal insulating garment. "You ready to go, Twist?" he asked.

"I am," Twistunder confirmed. "May I mount now?"

"Sure thing," Mack said and made as if to kneel down.

"No, no," Twistunder said quickly. "I am not injured, you know."

Human Friend Mack smiled and remained standing as Twistunder climbed up the back of his legs and settled himself onto Mack's shoulders. Mack opened the outer door and stepped out into the brilliant purple light of day. Mack slipped his ocular radiation shields over his eyes and began humming.

"Why does your confidence signaling increase when you put those on?" Twistunder asked as he traced the flushes of light up and down Human Friend Mack's neck and scalp.

"Because these are very cool sunglasses," Human Friend Mack explained as he picked up his particular stick from where the so-called 'walking sticks' leaned against the outer wall of the bio-dome.

"I did not know they assisted with thermoregulation," Twistunder said, very deliberately pitching his voice to mild innocence.

Human Friend Mack gave an explosive blast of air out of his nose, and his stripes rippled with humor. "I know you know what that word means," he said in a scolding tone. Meanwhile, he had slipped from the more agile stride he used in enclosed spaces to the energy-saving lope that he used to cover long distances.

"I do," Twistunder admitted. "But you still haven't answered my question."

"What question?" Human Friend Mack asked between long, deep breaths.

"Why are you out here expending calories when you have already gotten enough exercise today?" Twistunder asked again.

"I just felt like a walk," Human Friend Mack replied. "The weather is good, and it isn't always."

"What benefit do you get from this walk?" Twistunder asked. "There is our socialization of course, but that could be better facilitated back at the nice, warm couch or in your room if you wished solitude."

"It's a walk," Human Friend Mack said. "I mean just look at that, will you?"

He swung his arm out to indicate the terrain around them. Twistunder studied it carefully. The ground rolled away in cold, dry hummocks. The surface was covered with a brittle pseudo-algae that glinted darkly purple in the harsh light from the triple stars overhead. The silicone-rich lifeform provided enough oxygen to make the planet barely habitable for the sentient species that had found it.

"I see the conditions that make this world a death trap," Twistunder finally said, pulling closer to the comforting warmth of his friend.

"If it's so bad, why are you here in the first place?" Human Friend Mack asked with a laugh.

"The high joining determined that if you podlings decided to set up a colony here, we at least needed a science outpost," Twistunder replied. "We found it first after all."

"Fair enough," Human Friend Mack said with a shrug.

The slope of the ground increased, and his stride shifted slightly to compensate. They were currently traveling along the path the humans' feet had trampled out between the main base and the power generators. The Undulates could travel nowhere else under their own power. The local flora would lacerate their appendages dangerously if they tried without protective armor. Of course the same applied to the humans, but they would not go out without their protective foot armor in any case.

Twistunder made a mental note to add the probability of lacerating ground foliage to the list of dangers they faced if the humans ever let them near Earth.

"But what is the purpose of this walk?" Twistunder pressed. "You are traveling too fast for exploration to be the goal."

"It's just a walk, Twist," he replied. "Fresh air—"

"We could open a window," Twistunder interjected.

"Exercise—" Human Friend Mack continued.

"You fulfilled twenty percent more than required in the gym this morning," Twistunder said.

"Companionship," Human Friend Mack went on.

"Equally available on the couch," Twistunder replied.

"It's tradition, Twist," Human Friend Mack said with a sigh. "It's just tradition."

They reached a hillock, and Human Friend Mack planted his walking stick in the ground to provide a third point of support and looked out over the iridescent purple plain. Twistunder took in the strange, low growing ecosystem for a moment and then left its contemplation to the human. Honestly the patterns that rippled over Human Friend Mack's skin were more interesting to him. Granted, he wasn't a field biologist. Fortunately these 'walks' gave them both a chance to indulge their observational interests. Perhaps that was the point after all.

Humans are Weird – Rituals

"Hey, Twist, bud," Mack Dodge called out from the open refrigeration unit, "have you seen the bottle of chilled acetone?"

The human continued to paw through the bright orange unit, causing a clacking of various containers and a rustling of sample bags. After a few moments passed with no response, he lifted his head from his search and stared across the small laboratory with an annoyed frown on his unshaven face.

"Twistunder!" Mack said with a bit of a snap in his voice. However, despite the display of irritation in the much larger human, the Undulate sat still on the counter that lined the far wall. Mack frowned and closed the unit. He walked towards his friend. "Twist," he said. "That was not a rhetorical question if you were wondering."

He frowned as he considered Twistunder. The Undulate had balled himself up in what Mack might have called a thinking loaf position, but something was different. All of Twist's many appendages were tucked tightly under him, too tightly. He looked less like a bread loaf and more like a bundle of rope someone had tightened too far.

"Twist?" Mack asked, real concern in his voice now. He reached out to touch the Undulate but hesitated. He instead held out his hand, palm down, and then violently twisted his fingers in a clockwise motion, moving his wrist as little as possible. Twist started, a tremor running through his body, before his gripping appendages appeared and reared up in a soothing greeting.

"Friend Mack," Twistunder said, his voice flat with distraction, "forgive me, I was lost in thought."

"You okay, bud?" Mack asked with a frown. "Are you dehydrated? Do you need a sink bath?"

"No, no," Twist assured him. "I am fine. I could use a drink though."

"Let me grab one for you," Mack offered. He scooped Twist up under his arm and headed for the commissary. An odd tremor, one the likes of which Mack had never felt before, ran through Twistunder's body, and the human glanced down at the Undulate in surprise. "Are you sure you're okay, Twist?" he asked again.

"I'm fine," Twist insisted. His voice was firm this time, showing that he was at least aware enough to give it human-specific emotional overtones. "I am just processing disturbing concepts."

"Ah," Mack nodded as they reached the now empty commissary, and he set Twist down on a chair. For some reason, laboratory counters were acceptable perches, but tables and other eating dedicated surfaces were not. Mack got a glass of water and brought it back to Twist, who gratefully dropped a few secondary appendages into it.

"Thank you, Friend Mack," Twist said as the water slowly drained out of the glass.

"So have you seen the acetone?" Mack asked.

"No," Twist replied. "But I did scent it in the upper cabinets."

"Thanks," Mack said, rising. "I'll just go get that and put it in the fridge to chill."

"Friend Mack," Twist asked as Mack reached the door. "Do you have a tattoo?"

"Yeah," Mack said with a grin. "I'll show you when I get back."

That same tremor went across Twist's body, and Mack

shrugged. He put the acetone in the fridge – what idiot left it in the cabinet anyway? – and strolled back to Twist.

"So tattoos," Mack said with a grin. He hiked his leg up on the chair and went to pull up his pants leg. However, Twist held out a gripping appendage and gently restrained his hand.

"Exactly what was the ink made of that was used for your markings?" Twist asked in an oddly neutral tone.

Mack arched an eyebrow at that. "Carbon black, iron oxide, and silver," he answered. "My parents insisted that if I wanted a tat, I learn everything about them."

"There is no ash in your particular tattoo?" Twist asked, letting a little eagerness slip into his tone.

"No," Mack said with a grin. "Old Man Kirkpatrick was trustworthy as they come. He would never cut his ink with anything and not label it."

"Oh, then I would very much like to see your body ornamentation," Twist said, perking up immediately and spreading out his appendages a bit.

Mack smiled and pulled his pants leg up and his sock down. Twist eagerly reached out his sensory appendages to examine and touch the small school of tropical fish inked in black on Mack's ankle.

"This is a lovely pattern," Twist said brightly. "Made of carbon black, you say?"

"Yes," Mack confirmed. "What did you think it was made of?"

Twist hesitated and pulled his appendages back to his sides. "Ah, I do not mean to offend, Friend Mack," Twist said. "Are you comfortable discussing human death rites?"

Mack let out a bark of laughter. "Sure thing, Twist," he assured him.

"Well," Twist said, "I was talking to Smith Three."

"Well, that explains things," Mack said, rolling his eyes. "Old Three is confusing as they get."

"He showed me his," Twist paused, and a shudder ran through his body again, and his voice went so flat it became hard for Mack to distinguish the words 'commemorative tattoo.'

"And what was the ink in Smith Three's tat made of?" Mack asked, guessing the source of Twist's discomfort.

"His grandfather," Twist said in that same flat tone.

Mack stared blankly at the Undulate, trying to parse his words. "You mean he said his grandfather made the ink?" Mack asked.

"No," Twist's voice seemed to grow stronger on seeing Mack's confusion. "The ink was made of his grandfather."

Mack stared at Twist long enough that Twist began to wave his gripping appendages.

"Does this disturb you, Friend Mack?" Twist asked.

Mack started; he wondered if the pleased eagerness in Twist's tone was deliberate. "That can't be right," Mack sputtered. "Humans don't... I mean not now... I mean how is that even possible?"

"Smith Three went into great detail," Twist shuddered again but not so strongly this time. "He described how the body was devoured by flames and reduced to carbon and calcium. Then the remains were powdered finely and mixed with the ink that was used to mark his skin."

Mack let out a low profanity. Neither Twist nor Smith Three was the kind to make something like this up.

"I take it you are disturbed," Twist stated.

"Ya' think?" Mack demanded.

"I do," Twist said in satisfaction. "May I sit in your lap and share your warmth and distress?"

"Sure, sure," Mack said with a sigh. "I need to finish the experiment but sure."

Twist scrambled across the space into his lap and settled into a more proper thinking loaf. Mack sighed and dropped a hand down to stroke his upper side.

"Ash," Mack muttered.

"Ash," Twist confirmed.

"Man, humans are strange," Mack observed.

"You said it," Twist agreed.

Humans are Weird – Didn't See it

"I had no intention at all to step on him," Smith sated. "Like I said, I just didn't see him."

"I know your vision is directional," Twistunder said, "but there was nothing in between your line of vision and Grrrwll."

"Yeah, but I wasn't… scanning?" Smith was clearly struggling for words.

"I seem to recall you expressing stress when you walked into a room under a similar situation," Twistunder pointed out. "You let out a howl of distress because you couldn't, and I quote, 'unsee what had been seen.'"

"Yes…" Smith said, running her eyes over Twistunder as if she could follow his logic with her selectively faulty vision.

"The implication was that you could not turn off your visual sense," Twistunder pressed.

"I can't," Smith affirmed. "But you know it's hard to process directional vision all the time. Sometimes I just want a break."

"Wait a moment," Twistunder tensed his appendages as he tried to process what the human had said. "You possess the ability to map out waveforms with specialized organs. With this ability you can make astounding scientific observations, take out opposing warriors by propelling rocks at them from a distance, and can judge the mood of fellows from across the room… and you sometimes walk into you crew members because you just *ignore* this sense?"

The human in front of him shifted uneasily on her bean bag and took a deep breath. "Well, yes, I just didn't see Grrrwll," Smith repeated.

Twistunder rubbed his gripping appendages together in frustration. This new species was decidedly confusing.

Humans are Weird – Here There Be Dragons

The humans on the base were excited. No one was particularly concerned about this fact yet. The planet they were on was mild even by the standards of the Undulates, who found a mere two degrees of temperature drift uncomfortable. The base was well built and meant to provide comfort and protection in equal parts. Most importantly the base commander was a Shatar with half a lifetime of experience dealing with human madness. All factors considered, the inhabitants of the base were interested and watchful.

Gc'ska had not yet determined what the humans were excited about, but the general emotional expressions were smiles and laughter and light steps, so he was hopeful that it was to be a pleasant surprise. Still, hope was one thing; evidence was another. Which was why he had sought out the apparent source of the expectation.

"Friend Helen," Gc'ska called out as he skittered up to her, all six of his motile legs working overtime to keep up with her bipedal stride. "May I speak to you?"

"Sure thing, Grits, buddy!" Helen called out.

There was bright energy in her voice, and Gc'ska felt his own spirits lift at the sound. He leapt eagerly into the hand she proffered and perched there as she brought him up to her face.

"What do you want to know?" she asked.

"It has been noted that the humans seem to be expecting something," Gc'ska pointed out. "I would like to know what you are anticipating."

"Well, Grits!" Helen said, her voice interrupted by a giggle. "We weren't sure it was going to work out, so we didn't say anything, but my request for a new pet finally came through."

"Ah," Gc'ska said, bringing his primary manipulators up to his mandibles. "A pet is a companion animal, yes?"

"Yep!" Helen said brightly. Her head nodded eagerly, and her brilliant gold head covering bounced entrancingly. "We don't dare bring any Earth creatures to this world. They would muck up the ecosystem pretty bad, so one of the domestication crews went out to the southern seas to look for something pet-worthy. Well, they found a nice, little warm-blooded lizard thing that fits all the criteria, and because it needs to be tested out on-planet before they go off world, this base and me..." her voice rose, and she skipped a little, "gets to test out the first pet-forms!"

"And this creature is arriving when?" Gc'ska asked cautiously. He knew what humans considered suitable pets.

"Now!" Helen nearly squealed out. "The crate is landing now."

Gc'ska realized that Helen's steps had taken them to the transport bay, and indeed there was a carrier drone approaching with a crate about the size of an Undulate. A low hiss came from the crate as it settled onto the reception platform.

"Uppsie!" Helen called out as she set Gc'ska on her shoulder. "I can't wait to see my new baby."

Gc'ska watched as she opened the crate and tenderly pulled out a horrifying creature of the abyss. Twin pairs of forward-facing hunter eyes blinked at him. *At him.* It seemed to be ignoring its new master as she cooed over it. Its well-defined, human-like muscles tensed and relaxed under its shimmering opalescent skin. The scales that covered the skin gave the beast a dark blue coloration that shifted as Helen stroked her hands over it.

"Isn't he adorable?" Helen crooned.

"Adorable," Gc'ska automatically agreed.

The animal flicked a forked tongue out of his mouth and pulled its lips back to reveal dozens of razor sharp teeth.

"Adorable," Gc'ska whispered as he slunk back under Helen's hair.

Humans are Weird – Those Were Warnings, Not Suggestions

"All non-classified data is to be placed on the shared drive," Forty-five Trills burst out. "That is clearly stipulated in the regulations!"

"How," demanded Ghas'tck, waving his primary manipulation appendages in frustration, "did you not think this needed to be classified?"

"I assumed this was already common knowledge among humans," Forty-five Trills defended himself.

Ghas'tck let his appendages drop down and rubbed his eyes in frustration. His rearmost motile appendages rubbed together, and he grimly felt the remaining numbness.

Forty-five Trills noticed the motion and drew his wings together in a sympathetic wince. "Is the flame damage healing well?" he asked.

"As well as can be expected," Ghas'tck stated. "Now, when did you first start compiling this..." he hesitated as he mulled over the proper descriptors, "this list?"

"It was soon after the first humans entered this sector," Forty-five Trills explained. "I was stationed on the observation platform that had been shared with the Shatar once. So it was the only base built to specs that could house a human. The rest were far too small. However, we had a mega-mite infestation on the base at the time."

"Sweet Mother Flight," Ghas'tck hissed. "Not the piercing kind?"

"Shedding no," Forty-five Trills replied with a shudder. "Just the daubing kind. But they were perhaps three times the size… so all around an uncomfortable experience when you come across something that is nearly your mass that looks so very much like the tales of a demon one hears of in pups' stories." He fluffed and smoothed his fur with a huff. "Well, we assumed that a predatory species of the human's mass would not be so concerned with their presence," he continued.

"And it was the only base there," Ghas'tck acknowledged.

"And it was the only base there," Forty-five Trills confirmed. "We warned them. We did warn them. I can only assume that the human in question failed to absorb the briefing entirely because it came out after the incident investigation that he had not seen one of the 'bleeding horrific giant buggers' before."

"But from your description, the mega-mites were a fraction of a hundredth of a human's mass," Ghas'tck replied.

"Indeed," Forty-five Trills replied. "In times since then, I have seen humans dispatch the same species with a mere flick of their hands. But apparently they have a preferred size for mites, and anything that dares to grow larger must be 'killed with fire.'"

"And so that is what the human on the base did?" Ghas'tck asked.

"Yes," Forty-five Trills said with a sigh. He ran his winghook over his sensory horns and stared glumly at the list Ghas'tck was displaying on the pad. "He found the main nest and improvised an incendiary device out of a pressurized can of cleaning solvent and the ignition factors of some outdated mining equipment," Forty-five Trills went on.

"Didn't his screaming alert you before the fact?" Ghas'tck demanded. "Human lungs are… powerful to say the least."

"I might remind you I had never experienced human behavior

before this," Forty-five Trills replied. "Even if I had, this particular human wasn't prone to screaming. We had no warning before the fire suppressant systems informed us of his tampering with them. Well, we followed the indicators and found him singed and satisfied."

"What did he say?" Ghas'tck asked with a feeling of macabre interest.

"Everything's fine now," Forty-five Trills replied. "Anyway, I had to write up the report for that incident, so I had that copy in my records. When it became clear that this wasn't a random encounter due to prolonged exposure to space but a standard reaction to unknown threats, I decided to keep the list. Most entries are from my official reports, some are from incidences I observed personally, and some are purely second-wing telling."

"And what was the purpose of this list?" Ghas'tck asked.

"Safety!" Forty-five Trills nearly shrieked out, flailing his wings wide. "I wanted every officer in charge of a human to be aware that given an immediate threat, an approaching threat, or an insufficiency of threats, a human's first response is to set something on fire! I wanted them to be able to react to that!"

Forty-five Trills lunged across the table and gripped Ghas'tck's head in his winghooks. Ghas'tck stiffened but didn't panic. They had worked together for too long for him to really fear the irritating Winged.

"How was I supposed to know?" Forty-five Trills demanded. "How was I supposed to know that a list made for warning purposes would be taken as a—" His voice broke out of Ghas'tck's hearing range, and the Trisk winced back for a moment.

"Control yourself, Forty-five Trills," Ghas'tck said firmly. "What did you say the list was taken as?"

Forty-five Trills dropped back to his seat and gave a groan.

"The humans took it for a challenge," he finally said weakly. "They print it out and check off the explosive, incendiary, and electric devices as they find ways to improvise them with the materials on hand."

"And that is why I was caught in that blast in the storage bay?" Ghas'tck asked.

"Human Green had found a new type of cleaning solvent," Forty-five Trills replied.

"This is all very interesting," Ghas'tck said, "and informative. However, the device that involved myself was not described in your list."

"I did mention the part where the humans improvise," Forty-five Trills pointed out.

"That you did," Ghas'tck said. "And now the list is out there and growing."

"Well, they survived long enough to achieve space flight," Forty-five Trills pointed out. "They can't be too careless with explosions, can they?"

Humans are Weird – Storm's A' Comin

"And was there any sign of these atmospheric disturbances before the mainframe crashed?" Twistunder asked.

"Nope," the human replied.

At least that was what Twistunder thought the human had said. The massive alien was curled over the side of one of the plasticized containers that housed the research base's computing nodes. Twistunder spread out his appendages and let the ambient atmospheric conditions fill his awareness. The moisture in the air was stable so far as he could tell. He would not need to moisturize for hours. The atmospheric currents were smooth and regular. He knew that his species really wasn't skilled in measuring such things, but he had learned a few tricks from the Trisk whom he had served with. All in all, there was no indication that anything was wrong.

"Why are you so concerned about the functionality of the sensor array then?" Twistunder asked.

"Those storms come up fast," the human replied. "We don't want to get caught out."

"Indeed," Twistunder muttered as he observed the human wrench out the damaged component with what looked like far more than necessary force.

The human focused his binocular vision on the component, and his face twisted into an expression of displeasure. Twistunder thought it had been damaged by electrical discharge, but that made no sense, and he was no engineer. The human was about to replace the component when he suddenly snarled and dropped the item. One hand was tightly gripping the other. Twistunder felt a wave of pain pheromones wash over him, and the fact that he could sense it at all in the thin atmosphere told him how extreme the human's pain must be.

Twistunder contemplated offering assistance, but the human suddenly straightened and slammed the top of the container shut. "We're leaving," the human said curtly.

"Of course," Twistunder said. "I will drive, and we will get back to the base to tend to your injury."

"What injury?" the human asked even as he proceeded to lock down the container.

"The one that caused you such pain just now," Twistunder replied.

The human chuckled and glanced over at Twistunder as he gathered up his tools. "I'm not injured," he said. But at that same moment, he grunted in pain and flexed his hand.

"I believe I have localized your injury," Twistunder said, reaching up for the jointed appendage.

The human snatched away his hand. "I am not injured!" he snapped. The human took a deep breath and tossed his tools back into the transport. "Seriously, little man. I am not injured. I'll explain on the way back to the base, but we need to leave now."

"Very well," Twistunder began.

The human bent down and scooped him up before tossing him into the travel couch and leaping into the control couch. Twistunder took a moment to secure his safety restraints as the human initiated the engines and headed towards the base at maximum acceleration.

"Why are we returning to base at an unsafe velocity?" Twistunder demanded.

"There's a storm coming," the human said in a low tone, flexing his hand.

Twistunder pondered this for a moment. "Pardon me," he said, "but I believe the reason that we came out here was because the predictive system for storms was nonfunctional."

"I don't need that fancy computer to tell me a storm's coming when it's this close," the human said. "My hand starts acting up. That was that pain you noticed."

"Your hand experiences pain when a storm happens?" Twistunder asked in confusion.

"Hurts like mad for a bit," the human said. "But it passes."

Twistunder couldn't think of a response, and after a moment the human grinned at him.

"It's a cartilage and bone thing," the human said. "And here it comes."

Twistunder was vaguely aware that the human had just accelerated the transport past the suggested limits, but he was focused on the western sky where the light of the sun was being blotted out by a sparking mass of chaos.

"Storm's a' coming," the human commented grimly.

Humans are Weird – Jump Scare

"Secondary Visiting Ranger?" Fourth Sister asked when she handed him the soil probe.

The brilliant yellow sun shone down on the frozen landscape. She would never have dared venture out onto such a place herself without the presence of a true mammal. Even with her insulation gear that muted the sounds of even loud conversation, she could already feel the air draining her core warmth. Fortunately humans were rather loud when it came to communication. Even so, the grunt the human gave in reply did not seem to contain any words, but she was learning that humans were rather imprecise when it came to casual verbal communication, so she took it to be permission to continue.

"Are you currently in a state of, ah, I believe the word is 'feud' with Primary Visiting Ranger?" she asked.

"Primary? Oh, you mean Bob?" the human asked.

"Yes," she replied.

The human took a moment to shift the hood of the parka he was wearing around his tiny audio sensors but did not expose the round little nubs of skin. "A state of feud?" His lips turned down in a gesture of either displeasure or thought. "Not that I know of. Why?"

"Well, given that he is about to—" Fourth Sister began.

The still, thick atmosphere was split by a high-pitched shriek as Primary Visiting Ranger leapt out from behind a shrubbery and grasped at Secondary Visiting Ranger. Fourth Sister felt her frill slapping against the interior of her thermal wear in confusion. Primary Visiting Ranger was perhaps a full body length from Secondary Visiting Ranger. There was no way a human could physically touch another from that distance. However, Secondary Visiting Ranger still leapt back with a vocalization that she was fairly certain counted as a profanity. She stooped over to pick up the probe Secondary Visiting Ranger had dropped.

"Really, Bob?" Secondary Visiting Ranger demanded, his hand clutched over his primary circulatory pump. "Really?"

Primary Visiting Ranger was laughing in delight to such an extent that Fourth Sister was somewhat concerned for his health. He doubled over and braced his arms on his knees. "Oh yeah, Mack," he finally gasped. "Really. You should have seen your face!"

"Real mature," Secondary Visiting Ranger muttered.

She could not see under his goggles, but from the flexing of the exposed muscles, she presumed that he was performing that odd ritual of 'rolling his eyes' that was so very disturbing. Inset organs should not move in that manner.

"Is this an amusing encounter or an antagonistic one?" Fourth Sister asked as she handed Secondary Visiting Ranger the soil probe.

"Amusing!" Primary Visiting Ranger stated firmly, all of his teeth showing in a wide grin.

"Not antagonistic," Secondary Visiting Ranger spoke at the same time. "Just annoying and immature."

"You needed the cardio anyway," Primary Visiting Ranger said. He straightened and strode past them, not breaking stride but managing to clout Secondary Visiting Ranger on the shoulder with those built-in clubs humans were so infamous for.

"See you back at the base, Mack," he said cheerfully.

"Not if I see you first," Secondary Visiting Ranger muttered.

Humans are Weird – Self Control

"For the record," Eighth Sister said as calmly as she could with her frill extended as far as it would go in a display she could only pray the human didn't recognize as scornful disbelief.

"For what record?" the human sitting across the table from her demanded. His outer membrane was flush with toxin signals, and his pheromone cloud was awash with horrid indicators of the internal torment his digestive system was going through. For once in her career, Eighth Sister regretted that human biosignals were so easy to translate.

"The medical record," Eighth Sister said, forcing her frill to lay flat. "The one your superiors are paying me to keep. The one that you yourself said was a, and I quote, 'Crackerjack—'"

"Don't quote my words back to me," snapped the human, slumping in a way that should not have been possible for a creature with a calciferous endoskeleton.

"Very well," Eighth Sister agreed. She reminded herself that the digestion-impeded human was suffering far more than she was and deserved sympathy. Even if, as she suspected, his suffering was entirely his own doing. "Now when you submitted your specific dietary needs to the base, you indicated that you had a dangerous learned immune response to what common human foods?" she asked.

"Gluten, mammalian lactation, and yeast byproducts," the human muttered with a sigh.

"And what product did you specifically order from the non-essential foodstuffs merchant?" she asked.

"Chocolate éclairs," the human said in a still lower voice.

"And did you personally eat these non-essential foodstuffs?" she asked.

"I bloody well did!" snapped the human. "For the record, you know."

"And what are the primary ingredients of these non-essential foodstuffs?" she pressed on, deciding to ignore the outburst.

"Sugar," he began, "and chocolate and baking soda and baking powder and water…"

"And?" she pressed.

"Milk, gluten, and yeast," he muttered, somehow managing to slump even lower in his seat, all the while maintaining a steady, resentful glare at a point right in between her eyes.

She waited for him to continue, to offer some explanation, but he only glared at her defiantly until she let her frill droop and gestured at the door. As he stood, his gastro system released a cloud of foul waste product, and he flushed in embarrassment before hurrying out of the room. Eighth Sister clamped down her frill and wondered if she could get a transfer.

Humans are Weird – Scary Story

"There is something wrong with the human," Twistunder announced as he slipped into the recreation pool.

"From your posture, I assume it is not the sort of wrong that requires immediate attention," Amblesover observed as he shuffled across the bottom of the pool, stirring the algal system with every lazily dragged nub.

"He is showing signs of sleep deprivation," Twistunder explained, "and his fight, flight, or freeze circuits are so dramatically over active that even I noticed them. He nearly screamed when I simply touched his hand from inside the cupboard."

"Did he give you any explanation?" Amblesover asked.

"Well, he did specifically request that I," Twistunder lifted himself vertical and hunched in the resentful air the human had taken, "should just leave him alone and mind my own business."

Amblesover hummed in sad sympathy, and the two Undulates circled each other in a comforting greeting before settling into the artfully arranged algal garden. Twistunder ran his primary appendages over the long, smooth tassels of an emerald green variety and let the warmth of the water soothe his gravity-stressed appendages. After several minutes had passed by, Amblesover lightly shoved him with a gripping appendage. Twistunder stiffened and edged just a thread's breadth away to indicate his indignation. He was trying to ease out a sulk here.

"Would you like to know what is wrong with the human?" Amblesover asked with mild amusement agitating his appendages.

"You do not even know what human I indicated," Twistunder pointed out, but he could not hide his curiosity.

"It doesn't matter," Amblesover said, taking off from the pool floor and waving an appendage dismissively as he swam around Twistunder. "It is the same for all of them."

"This is a base-wide problem?" Twistunder asked.

If true, that did relieve his distress about his particular friend even if it did raise other issues.

Amblesover rotated his appendages in a gesture that had been heavily influenced by the human shrug and climbed up onto a sunning rock. "I don't know if you could call it a problem exactly," he said in slow, musing tones.

Twistunder tightened his stance in annoyance. "How is – according to you – the entire human population of the base displaying signs of fear stressors not a problem?" Twistunder demanded.

Amblesover hummed in amused patience and stretched out against the gravity. "Do you recall all the hubbub over the so-called predator practice?" Amblesover asked.

"I do," Twistunder confirmed. "Tag, I think the humans called it."

"Do you recall what the Shatar were so concerned about?" Amblesover prompted.

"I fail to see the connection between that and this!" Twistunder said.

Amblesover prodded him with a gripping appendage.

"Very well," Twistunder muttered. "I will follow your wake. The Shatar recognized the behavior as practice of endurance predation as observed in several non-sapient deathworld species. They were concerned that there was some factor in the base environment that was stimulating the human to such an extreme behavior."

Amblesover waved for him to go on.

"The conclusion of the investigation showed that it was simply a childhood gaming behavior," Twistunder continued, "albeit one that was the result of the human's ecological past of being endurance pursuit predators."

"The humans were exposing their bodies to the conditions that they might have to encounter to maintain their physical strength through play behavior," Amblesover summarized as he leisurely stretched his non-gripping end into the water. "And so is it any surprise they also do so with their awareness?"

Twistunder slumped in blank bemusement, and Amblesover rolled into the water in a deliberate display of humor.

"The humans are in the process of testing each other's psychological toughness," Amblesover explained. "The process also strengthens their psychological toughness."

Twistunder slowly bobbed his gripping end in a rough approximation of a nod. "That does explain the symptoms I have seen in my human friend," he said slowly. "But why have I not observed the practice itself, and why are they suddenly doing it now?"

"They do it at night," Amblesover explained. "And they trek inland into the dry highlands where we can't go."

"Do they wish to hide this behavior from us?" Twistunder asked, twisting his appendages in distress at the thought.

"Far from it," Amblesover said, waving an appendage dismissively. "But to answer both questions, the conditions the practice is performed over preclude our presence. They like to be high and dry... there is usually an open flame and copious consumption of alcohol. Therefore, they prefer these dry summer months."

"That does sound particularly horrid," Twistunder said with a shudder. "What could they be possibly doing under those conditions that counts as play and then leads to those mental states?"

"They're telling scary stories."

Humans are Weird – Noping Out of There

"I'll see you tomorrow," Ryan called out as he shrugged into his jacket.

"You gonna ask what's up with that?" the receptionist asked, jerking her chin to the slow-flowing stream that took up the far side of the corridor.

Ryan glanced where she indicated and smiled ruefully. One of the younger Undulates was poking its gripping end out of the stream and very obviously waiting for attention. There had been a campus-wide memo about not disturbing the staff during working hours, and the Undulates were still smarting a bit from the sarcasm that had saturated the note.

Ryan strolled over and waved in greeting at the Undulate, who flung its body into a gleeful rotation greeting. Ryan had being taught that a double twist like that translated roughly to, 'Goody, goody, goody, I was noticed!' He laughed in delight and knelt, holding out his hand. The Undulate scrambled out of the water and rushed forward to press into his palm.

Greetings, Human Coworker Ryan, it pressed into his hand. *Was your diurnal cycle satisfactory? Please speak to me. I am learning.*

"Very much so," Ryan replied, pressing and speaking at the same time.

Are you well-rested? it asked.

"Well enough," Ryan said. "Who are you exactly?" He had found it was far better to risk the offense of exposing your own ignorance than to risk the offense of being wrong about who you were talking to.

The Undulate quickly backed off, and for a moment Ryan was concerned, but then the Undulate, fluffed up with pride, spoke. "I am waiting to be named!" he said.

"Ah," Ryan nodded sagely as the Undulate bumped back into his hand. "Smart move." That phrase translated very well thankfully. "I waited for my movement name too. What is your movement name?"

The Undulate writhed in a hopelessly complex movement that sent it skittering across the solid floor. Ryan couldn't help bursting out into laughter.

"Well then, Tapsalot," he said cheerfully. "What did you want to talk to me about?"

Tapsalot paused, and for a moment only his gripping appendages continued to tap in thought against the floor. Finally he scrambled back to Ryan's hand.

You are a botanist, correct? he asked.

"I've been known to study a few plants," Ryan said.

Would you like to enjoy a semi-recreational activity with me in relation to our mutual field of study? Tapsalot asked. His body was tense with eager anticipation, and Ryan grinned.

"Sure, little guy," he replied. "I've got nothing better to do this afternoon. What did you have in mind?"

I have heard that humans have a custom whereby they travel some distance to observe the temporal chromatic alterations in the local flora biomes, Tapsalot explained, falling back from the purposely casual language he had been using to the University Standard. *There will be a change in a nearby floral mass, caused by it switching from a vegetative to a reproductive state, and I wished to know if you would attend with me at diurnal hour seven point three-six. We would leave the transport hub at diurnal hour six,* Tapsalot paused and then switched back to the common language, *six and a

191

quarter.*

"I'd love to," Ryan said with no little surprise. He hadn't heard of any foliage worth watching around the rocky island the University was situated on. There were copious amounts of ground cover, but the lack of seasons on this planet meant all changes were gradual and essentially random.

His train of thought was derailed as Tapsalot rolled sideways in glee before very obviously gathering himself together and shuffling back to Ryan with assumed dignity. *I will meet you at the transport surface marked with the number four and the letter h,* Tapsalot told him.

"Will do, little guy," Ryan called.

Ryan went back to his dorm room and changed into clothes that could stand a trip outside. He grabbed his datapad on local ecosystems and strolled outside. The streams that the Undulates used in the place of sidewalks were only about a meter wide, and he normally leapt over them without thought, but today he took the zigzagging route over the foot bridges. He had plenty of time, and the weather was comfortably warm. It was a perfect afternoon for a walk. The triple suns gleamed down through the ice-dense atmosphere. The sky was gleaming down in a swirl of muted rainbows, and the network was washing against the shore of the island in gentle waves. He paused under the sadly spindly pine tree and stared ruefully down at the circle of dying ground cover around it. It really did look like the more acidic earth fauna wouldn't be allowed.

"You're just too much for this ecosystem, bud," Ryan reached out and patted the rough bark. "Don't worry. We still love you back home, and besides, there isn't enough wind on this world for you to develop proper branches anyway."

He finally reached the transport field and tossed his backpack into the hover that was waiting there. It was oblong somewhat like a surfboard with raised edges and a textured surface. There were a few jeeps over in one corner. But the wheeled vehicles got almost no use in this mild atmosphere, and he was rather fond of the 'magic-carpet' feel of the Undulate transports.

Greetings, Human Coworker Ryan, Tapsalot called out from the stream that led into the transport hub.

"Howdy, Tapsalot," Ryan called out.

The Undulate heaved itself out of the water and shuffled across the ground in what was a pretty brisk trot for the breadbox-sized folk. Ryan waited patiently by the transport until Tapsalot paused by the transport.

"Are we ready to go?" Ryan asked.

Tapsalot waved an appendage in agreement and ambled up onto the transport, taking the position near the leading point. The controls rose out of the textured material like nodes forming from bark. Ryan climbed up behind him and mentally prepared himself for the slow drift. The transport rose to about a meter over the ground and smoothly accelerated to a brisk jogging pace.

"How does the name I suggested feel now that you have had a chance to try it out?" Ryan asked.

Tapsalot gave an excited wriggle of his gripping end that indicated he was well pleased but didn't bother trying to speak over the wind. When he had calmed down somewhat, he raised a single gripping appendage from the controls and indicated the northern sky. Ryan first squinted in that direction and then relaxed his focus, but he couldn't see anything in particular.

"What's over there?" he asked.

Relevant weather patterns to the foliage change, the Undulate's non-gripping end explained.

Ryan nodded, trusting that the eyeless alien was seeing

something in the atmosphere that he wasn't, and then leaned back on his hands. It wasn't particularly far to the little cove where they were headed. The transport pulled up to where the smooth, glossy marine ground cover met the water, and Ryan and Tapsalot strolled out onto the slick beach analog created by the water formations on this planet.

"Ya know," Ryan offered as Tapsalot led him to a convenient place to sit and observe, "our water formations are a lot different back home."

As are ours, Tapsalot agreed. *Our surface is covered in great coral forests and wide-spreading waters. These deep, narrow canyons are quite strange, aren't they?*

"Wouldn't call them canyons myself," Ryan observed. "I haven't see one that's more than a foot above the water level even at low tide."

What would you call them? Tapsalot asked, managing to put a note of curiosity in the sound of his voice.

"Oh, the folks back at Central University are deciding on a proper word for them," he replied. "For now we just call them the narrows."

He spotted a seed pod from one of the larger plants that grew on this world and grinned. He stooped and picked up the pod while Tapsalot watched in interest. Ryan balanced the rounded disc in his hand for a moment before snapping it across the surface of the narrow. It skipped seven times before smacking into the far shore. Tapsalot was speechless for a moment, his body limp with astonishment. Ryan strolled over to the edge of the narrow and glanced down into the slightly murky water.

"Man, the diatoms are really going wild this season," he observed.

There was silence from behind him, but Tapsalot had gotten

over his shock enough to start toward their viewing location. He felt a small attention tap on his back, and Ryan glanced at Tapsalot.

Was that an example of human throwing? Tapsalot asked, his body held at an astonished angle.

"Sort of. I guess?" Ryan replied. "It is called skipping. Here we are." They plopped down on the bank, and Ryan gazed down into the water. "Are we looking at any particular species?" he asked.

There were quite a few flora-type species in the shallow grotto. Green tendrils waved over rust red coral growths. Light blue starbursts scattered in small clusters closer to the surface. The pink and blue ground cover that favored the edges of the narrows grew right down into the water for nearly a meter.

Tapsalot slipped into the water and swam down to a network of fine black threads that Ryan had taken for dead matter off of the green tendrils. Tapsalot swam back up with a sample and placed it in Ryan's hand. It really wasn't much thicker than a human hair. Ryan pulled out his multi-tool and examined the growth nodes while Tapsalot explained its reproductive strategy. The suns warmed the ground, and the water lapped leisurely at their appendages. Ryan kicked off his shoes.

"My eyes can't see much color in this," Ryan finally observed. "What color was it before?"

It hasn't changed yet, Tapsalot explained. *That is what we are here for. The reproductive effort change.*

"Oh," Ryan blinked. "So it all happens in one evening?"

For each individual, yes, quite quickly. Tapsalot pressed, *Is it not the way on Earth?*

"Not for the big popular foliage changes," Ryan said. "It takes many days if not weeks."

Fascinating! Tapsalot said. *How do the vegetative bodies capture hosts then?*

***

"What now?" Ryan asked.

Some sudden movement caught his eye, and he stared blankly at the water for a moment. The thin, black threads were writhing suddenly, frothing the water. Then they grew. They grew thick. They grew long. They grew many. They grew up.

"Nope!" Ryan sprang up and backed away.

Human Coworker Ryan? Tapsalot waved at him.

"Nope, nope, nope," Ryan expanded as the suddenly forty-meter-long tendrils reached for *him*.

He felt something cold and wet clinging to his hand. He glanced at the tendril he was holding and frantically tried to shake it off. It gripped like cold, wet glue – he ripped it off and tried to shake it off his fingers only to see it snatched away by the whole tendrils.

I do not comprehend your motion language, Human Coworker Ryan, Tapsalot waved at him.

The tendrils were reaching for the little Undulate.

"Nope. Out!" Ryan yelped. He dove forward and snatched up his friend. He sprinted to the transport and slammed his fist into a slight bulge on the rear.

Human Coworker Ryan! You just destroyed the speed and altitude limiter! Tapsalot pressed, hooting in sudden shock.

"You choose now to freak out?" Ryan demanded as he threw the transport into drive and sped away from the tendrils. More were popping up now all around them. Ryan lowered the sensitivity of the steering and began simply using his weight to shift their trajectory.

There was no reason to bread before! Tapsalot insisted.

"What? Never mind! We are almost clear," Ryan shouted.

Tapsalot fell silent and stayed that way.

"You okay, Friend Tapsalot?" Ryan asked, craning his head around to get a look at the Undulate, who was clinging to his back.

I humbly request that you green on the trajectory you are currently pursuing at velocities that will result in injury even to your internals if you carbon, Tapsalot pressed.

"Back skin isn't much good for translation," Ryan observed, "I'm pretty sure I felt a few of those words wrong, but I get the idea."

He fell silent and focused on getting them home. They pulled into their parking spot, and Ryan took a deep breath. Tapsalot climbed down in front of him and lifted his gripping appendages entreatingly.

Your pheromone profile suggests you were deeply frightened by the foliage change, Human Friend Ryan? Tapsalot said carefully.

"Well, I was," Ryan said, rubbing his face ruefully. "A cold, fast ride back gave me time to think about how you wouldn't have put yourself or me in a really dangerous situation."

Ah! Tapsalot wriggled in the apparently universal mix of shame and glee scientists experienced when they got amazing data from a fellow creature's suffering. *The famous human fight/flight/freeze response being constrained by reason!*

Ryan stared down at him with twitching lips and then burst out laughing. Tapsalot waited patiently for the outburst to end and shuffled forward with his gripping appendages up.

Shall we engage in the human comfort gesture known as cuddling, Human Friend Ryan? Tapsalot asked.

Ryan chuckled and held out his arms. Tapsalot climbed up and did his best friendly cat impersonation.

"Come on, bud," Ryan said, patting his new friend. "I need to report mauling a transport to the base mechanics."

Humans are Weird – Trees are for Climbing

Seven Trills fluttered along the outdoor recreation area just over the soft green ground cover as he listened to his assistant. The larger Winged was going over the list of guests that would be attending the opening of the new consulate. Seven Trills tried to pay attention, but the scorching heat of Sol was stinging his sensory horns dreadfully. He wondered how his assistant was ignoring it. He angled himself over to one of the solitary trees the humans kept in the area, hoping for shade. His assistant followed willingly, and Seven Trills soon perched on an exposed root in the clear area around the tree's base.

"And I think it would be best if we instituted a general search protocol to avoid insult to the delegate," his assistant said.

"Oh, yes, yes," Seven Trills replied.

His assistant was annoyingly persistently right about these things. The protective shade provided by the tree was suddenly disturbed by a movement in the branches overhead, and both Seven Trills and his assistant angled their eyes up to see what had made the disturbance in the oppressively still air.

"Is that a human?" Seven Trills asked.

"Is that human spying on us?" his assistant demanded.

Seven Trills heaved a sigh and took flight. His assistant followed.

"How would he know we would come to this tree?" Seven Trills asked.

"Ping," the assistant granted him.

They had now reached the human, and any question was put to rest. The human had braced his massive form against the trunk and branches and was blissfully sleeping away. His arms were sprawled over other branches. Seven Trills grabbed a handy perch and swung down to a resting position. His assistant joined him shortly.

"I don't think we should risk waking him," his assistant said in a tone they had determined humans couldn't hear.

"A fall from this height would be disastrous for a human," Seven Trills said.

What the human was doing here at all was the question.

"I checked the duty roster against his name," the assistant said after a moment spent working at his tablet. "This human is in a rest and recreation period, but due to the increased security, he can't leave the base."

"Bored humans," Seven Trills suggested.

"The base has more entertainment options than any of the surrounding communities," his assistant pointed out.

At this point the human's heart rate accelerated in the way that usually proceeded waking, and both Winged fell silent. The human twitched, stretched, and yawned. His eyes opened, revealing interwoven blue and green irises contrasting his deep black pupils. The colorful muscles dilated and contracted a few moments before he focused on them.

"Hey," the human said, pulling his lips up in a smile.

"Greetings," Seven Trills said. "Perhaps you can satisfy our curiosity."

"Sure?" the human replied.

"What are you doing up here?" the assistant demanded.

The human glanced down at the ground far below and then up at him. His face seemed to pass between confusion and curiosity a few times, and then he showed all of his teeth.

"Trees are for climbing, little friend. Trees are for climbing."

Humans are Weird – Medical Attention

"Never again."

The deeply distressed groan clearly came from a human voice, and Fifth Sister felt her frill twitch uneasily. She carefully placed the deep tissue sampler she had been tuning beside its mates in the case and shut it firmly. She rose from her perch and faced the door with all the dignity she could muster. Being the youngest xeno-medic ever to have graduated from the Central University was an honor to her family, but it did leave her feeling out of her depth among the humans. Quite literally, she mused as First Engineer staggered around the corner and approached her.

"Need anti-inflammatory stuff," he muttered with a slurred voice.

"That may be," she said, stiffening her frill in a display of firmness. "However, as I have told you before, I need to properly diagnose you."

The human groaned and muttered something about nosey medics before easing down into the diagnostic chair. Fifth Sister stood across from him and began the usual questioning even as she attached the skin sensors to his inflamed surface. She marveled anew at how much damage the human skin could take as the sensors clung to the clearly unhealthy surface. She caught a glimpse into the cavern of his mouth, and her frill rippled in shock.

"It appears that your mandible protuberances are loose," she said.

He replied with a low-grade profane statement that she had learned meant that he agreed with her diagnosis and considered it too obvious to bear restating.

"It appears that your mandible is rejecting your native—"

"It's just an allergic reaction!" he snapped. "I just need the usual stuff. The last medic just gave it to me."

"That would be against regulations," Fifth Sister said, trying to put sternness into her voice.

"Just get on with it," he muttered, rotating his eyes away as he slumped in that nearly Undulate way in the chair.

Fifth Sister looked at his medical history and clicked her mandibles. It did indeed look like this was a common occurrence for First Engineer. There was a justification for simply administering the known antidote for the allergic reaction. The diagnosis however caught her attention. She tilted her head and turned to the human.

"Why," she asked in a very non-threatening tone, "is the cause of your recurring medical issue listed as stupidity?"

The human gave a bark of laughter and grinned up at her, revealing his swollen internal tissues and that strange internal appendage prodding at his loosened protuberances.

"Look, I just broke down and ate some pizza, okay?" he said. "Got a little dairy, and I'm reacting."

"You file states—" she began.

"Yeah, yeah," the human waved her off. "Like my files says. Immature behavior, lack of self control, no intention for self-harm, i.e., stupidity. Just make your diagnosis and give me the dermal spray."

Fifth Sister agreed and determined to check his age against the human maturity charts. Surely a fully grown human wouldn't deliberately ingest a known poison.

Humans are Weird – Volcanoes

"Commander," the Investigator ran his primary leg over his optic frills in exasperation, "I freely acknowledge that your authority on this mission is nearly absolute."

The larger and more powerful Commander bristled in agitation and pulled his legs in stiffly in anticipation of a reprimand. The Investigator fought down a chitter of exasperation and turned his attention briefly to the report in his secondary leg to gather his thoughts. The small tent they were currently in flapped in the breeze, and the Investigator wondered at the strange structure. This entire situation was… odd. The exploration of the newly discovered planet was supposed to have been a reward to one of the Cluster's most distinguished warriors. A restful examination of a world that the smooth-headed elders of the Cluster had no real expectation of winning. True, this new species added a new complication, and they *had* landed disturbingly close on the same landmass. But none of that explained Commander Trill'th's bizarre behavior. The only thing that stood between Trill'th and a court-marshal at this point was his sterling record. No one in the Cluster hierarchy wanted to believe that the Hero of Tsoons was capable of treason.

"Now you say that turning control of the main computer nodes over to the technician from the human camp was justified due to the threat of imminent death to both your crew and the crew of the Flighted?" the Investigator asked.

"It is all in my report," Commander Trill'th hissed in irritation.

"Yes, yes," the Investigator agreed, "but I am afraid that the death of your Archivist has left the state of the records quite disordered."

Trill'th twitched his mandibles in agreement, and grief flicked across his eyes. The Investigator decided to put that investigation to the side for the moment. Exposure was the only listed cause of death, and the genuine terror, confusion, and sadness he had observed in the crew led him to believe that what had happened to the young clerk was indeed an accident.

"I simply wanted to clarify—" the Investigator was interrupted as a loud clicking alarm snapped through the air.

The Commander reacted without hesitation, darting from the tent at full speed to investigate the alarm. The Investigator suppressed another irritated chitter and began to gather his papers back into his carrying case. He arranged it on his back and followed the path of the Commander out, tasting the fear-spiked pheromones Trill'th had left on the pads of his motile legs. He found the Commander and the rest of the surviving officers clustered at the edge of the absurdly tall security fence. The crew was focused on a rapidly approaching figure. From the well-beaten path that led out across the grassy plain away from the camp, this was a well-used route. Almost a full road if it wasn't for the lack of pavement. But the size of the approaching vehicle was explanation enough for the size.

"That is a human," the Investigator observed in what he hoped was a neutral voice as he reached the cluster of officers.

"Sergeant Angelo," Commander Trill'th informed him curtly. "Male, barely into prime breeding age, generally friendly, and very open to interspecies interaction."

"And is that one of those helicopters you mentioned?" the Investigator asked. He knew very well that it wasn't, but the exasperated looks he received told him that the ploy had worked. A display of ignorance not specific to one's line of work made others see one as less of a threat.

"It's a motorcycle," one of the technicians informed him. "The interesting thing? Even though it has no gyroscopic balance system, it stays upright. The human has to constantly keep adjusting his position to maintain velocity."

The Investigator signaled his understanding and approached the Commander directly. "Are you going to let him into the camp?" the Investigator asked quietly.

"Yes," Trill'th answered in a flat tone.

"What security measures are you taking?" the Investigator asked cautiously.

Trill'th spun on him and raised his primary manipulating legs aggressively. "Letting the human in *is* a security measure."

The Investigator carefully kept his body language neutral. "How so?"

"Do you see the flag on the back of the motorcycle?" Trill'th demanded.

The Investigator turned his eyes towards the approaching machine and its giant rider. "I do," he agreed.

"It reflects light in the six hundred nanometer range. That means that whatever news he brings, ignoring it could kill us!" the Commander snarled.

The Investigator signaled his assent carefully. This situation was clearly beyond his current understanding, and he needed more information before he acted. The motorcycle drew closer, and the tension was rising in the small cluster when the ground began to shake. The Investigator stiffened and looked around frantically. The cluster tightened around him, and the Commander rested a comforting leg on his head.

"Steady," the Commander warned.

"What is that to the south?" one of the lesser officers demanded.

They all turned and began to chitter as they saw the growing plume of…something.

"Is that smoke?" the Investigator asked, fighting back his terror.

"The human probably knows," Trill'th offered. "It is unlikely that the red flag and this are unrelated."

"He has stopped!" the Investigator observed.

"The ground movement must have interfered with his movement," Trill'th speculated.

The giant biped was indeed stopped. He – if the Commander was correct on the human's sex – was standing on the still rolling ground, easily holding up the weight of the two-wheeled machine. The Investigator felt a thrill of unease at the casual display of raw strength. The human – Sergeant Angelo – made a few quick movements, and the motorcycle was left standing on its own while he switched out the so-called red flag with one that appeared to reflect in the high five hundred nanometer range. The small cluster visibly relaxed, and the Investigator looked to the Commander for explanation, lightly tapping the Commander's optic frills for an explanation.

"That is an orange flag," Trill'th explained. "It signifies a lesser but still potentially deadly threat."

"He has slowed," the Investigator observed.

"Whatever that," Trill'th waved to the growing pillar of... something… "was, it might have been far worse. He was coming to warn us of it. I assume you cut off outside communication when you arrived?"

"As is protocol," the Investigator replied uneasily.

"Well, you didn't get us killed," chattered the Commander. "Let's go find out what horror the humans are intimately aware of this time."

The Investigator signaled his assent as they moved towards the gate. Perhaps the fearsome reputation that preceded the humans was less fiction than he had presumed. That aside, he glanced nervously at the billowing pillar of smoke-like substance; the Commander's strange orders were beginning to seem more likely to be legitimate. They would have to wait and see. The motorcycle rolled to a stop outside the gate, and the human strode in as it opened for him.

"That was some volcano, hey?" he asked, flashing his teeth at them widely as he pulled up the protective coverings that had been shielding his luminous tri-colored eyes. "Hey – what?"

The cluster sprinted forward and raced up the giant biped's legs to perch on his shoulders. The Investigator followed along, observing carefully. The human tensed – what was visible of his soft supple skin grew tight – and then relaxed as the individuals of the cluster stilled and clung to him.

"So… never seen an eruption before, eh?" the human asked.

"Angelo," the Commander demanded in the human's language, running out onto the human's arm so he could stare into the human's newly revealed eyes, "what in the name of the Home Cluster was that?" He waved at the still growing plume.

"Just the planet releasing some pressure," the human answered. "We were worried it might be real big though. Barring any other information, it should be fine now. Good for the scientists, and no one died, right?" The human flashed his teeth again.

The Investigator wondered if that was supposed to be a comforting gesture as the Commander worked to get more specific details out of the human. The Commander's behavior was odd, but if the planet itself was flinging smoke into the sky… The Investigator shuddered as the human swayed in response to the ground moving again. He somehow doubted that he would be able to justify persecuting Trill'th.

Humans are Weird – Colonel

Twenty-seventh Cousin stared at the datapad in front of her and laid her dusky orange frill down tight against her neck. She rattled her mandibles together and finally leapt up from her crouch. She would simply have to find a human. She stepped out of her office and flicked her frill in companionable frustration at the other Twenty-seventh Cousin stationed in this one small college. She returned the greeting with her green frill.

"Have you seen any humans?" Twenty-seventh Cousin asked, fluttering her frill to indicate a very recent time frame.

"Second Brother is repairing the ground transports in the mechanical bay," the other Twenty-seventh Cousin replied.

"Gratitude," Twenty-seventh Cousin bobbed her body respectfully and stepped out lightly.

She found the human exactly where she had been told. Bent in a nearly Undulate manner into the engine compartment of the boxy green ground transport. She was about to greet him but caught a glimpse of his base defensive covering and clicked in annoyance at the stitched markers on the arm guards. Humans did not use the same naming system they did. That is why she was here after all. She pulled up the translation screen and readied the sound file she needed. She waited until his head was out of the metal chamber before tapping her talons lightly on the concrete floor.

"Hey!" he glanced over at her, and his strange, fleshy face contorted in that hilarious motion called a grin even as he wiped his stubby hands on a bio-fiber rag. "Tenth Sister, right?"

"I am Twenty-seventh Cousin," she said, lowering her frill in disapproval at the attempted flattery.

"Right, right," he said. "Which one now?"

"The linguist," she replied. "And you are Private Grimes."

"I never denied it!" he said with another grin.

She paused a moment, tilting her head to the side as she parsed her question. "Are you capable of aiding me with a matter of translation?" she finally asked.

"I can speak English pretty good," he said.

She tried not to leap back in shock when his primary arm attachment joints suddenly shifted up several inches. Were humans even attached under that pliable skin? She shook off the discomfort and held up the datapad.

"How do you pronounce this word?" she asked.

He leaned forward and his strange internal eyelids compressed. "Colonel," he said firmly.

She lowered her frill in a clear sign of aggravation that he actually responded to. Stepping back with a sudden change to a clearly defensive stance. She forced herself to relax.

"You have not offended me," she quickly informed him. "I have simply reached an impasse in my work."

"Ah," his head bobbed loosely on his thick neck. "So what's the problem?"

"Where is the," she pressed the recording so that the sound she wanted to enunciate played, "sound in this word?"

He gave a laugh and started to point, but the sound and the gesture broke off midway. His face contorted, and his eyelids blinked rapidly. The flesh flaps covering his teeth opened and closed several times, and he slowly withdrew his indicating finger.

"I don't know," he whispered in confusion. "Where is the 'r' sound in colonel?"

Humans are Weird – What's the Word

Quilx'tch tried not to slump with irritation as he followed his agitated colleague down the hall to the primary computer banks. The mix of bovine protein he was experimenting with had almost reached the temperature point just before boiling when he was forced by professional courtesy to prematurely end the experiment. Of course he could always heat the substance again, but his human contact assured him that this would cause molecular level disfigurement that would completely ruin the final consistency of the desired product.

Quilx'tch shot a glance at the hindlegs of his colleague and surreptitiously triggered the recording function of his tablet. "Call Pélé about possible workarounds for cheesecake recipe," he softly clicked.

"Are you paying attention?" his colleague demanded.

"Not entirely," Quilx'tch admitted. "Not until we get to the screens where I can actually see the evidence."

His colleague bristled in annoyance but waved a manipulator in acceptance of his logic.

"You say you have proof of various humans displaying this behavior more than once?" Quilx'tch asked in an attempt to get his mind focused.

"No," his colleague flicked his back leg in correction. "I only managed to record the behavior once. However, I have notes on the majority of similar cases."

"I have far too much experience with our newest biped friends," Quilx'tch began, "to ask why you do not simply describe the behavior."

"Thank you," the other replied, relaxing a little as they entered the comfortable-sized room built just for Trisk bodies and minds.

"However, why did you not just play the video on our mobile devices?" Quilx'tch asked as his colleague waved him over a three-dimensional display.

"Given that the behavior does not appear to be conscious, I thought it best to avoid any shame reactions if it is noted," his colleague explained.

"When have you ever," Quilx'tch demanded, "seen one of these space-faring humans display a shame reflex?"

"Look," his colleague pointed to the display as it began to play. "Just watch the human."

Quilx'tch bristled himself a bit at the rudeness but focused on the scene.

The human was 'sitting' at his work station while several Trisk worked around him. The massive human desk providing for nearly twenty Trisk work clusters. The human was poised in a position that Quilx'tch had come to associate with maximum productivity. His internal skeleton held the massive mammalian muscles rigidly up, and his fingers flew over the interface surface. From the looks of it, the high-ranking Ranger was composing a final report from all of the field data gathered on the economically vital 'space whales.' Suddenly however the rapid tapping of the human's fingers faltered and paused.

Quilx'tch titled his head in interest.

The human pulled his flexible upper lip in between his gleaming white teeth and chewed on it a moment, causing Quilx'tch to flinch in distress. One hand slid off of the active surface and began tapping idly on the desk frame, sending tremors through the superstructure that called the attention of all the Trisk present to the unconscious human.

"Gcas'kt!" the human suddenly called out.

Quilx'tch bristled a bit at the rudeness of the sudden interruption. He knew humans were abrupt, but this one did not even lift his eyes to the Trisk he addressed.

"Keep watching," his colleague muttered.

Quilx'tch obeyed.

"What is that word?" the human demanded.

Presumably of Gcas'kt. The main structure of the human's dominant arm was now pointed in the general direction of the Trisk who had first responded, but the hand was twisting around in a circular gesture that caused the pointing finger to encompass three-fourths of the room.

"That word that means how things, you know, how things go... go together. But fancy for the report..."

The various Trisk were now glancing at each other in confusion.

"Dynamics!" the human suddenly shouted. His hands immediately began flying across the active screen, and he grinned in delight. "Thanks, Gcas'kt!" the human called out.

After a long pause, one Trisk raised a manipulating appendage in confused consent. "You are welcome?" he replied.

"You're the best, lil bud," the human said.

The replay ended, and Quilx'tch looked into his colleague's eyes with resigned confusion.

"I have no comments to add to your research," Quilx'tch stated firmly.

Perhaps if he hurried, he could save his cheesecake.

Humans are Weird – Because

For a species that held the record for the greatest centralized mass of any known sapient, humans were sometimes extremely difficult to find. Rollsslowly pulled out his data unit and pressed it into one of the communications nodes. He sent out the inquisitive hum and again received the negative reply.

"So the human," Rollsslowly said to no one in particular, "is on the base—"

"Or at least his data unit is," offered a passing scientist.

"This world might not be as hostile to them as it is to us," Rollsslowly protested, "but Human Friend Steve is very cold sensitive. He would not have left the base."

"Your only options are to wait for his dedicated nutrient ingestion time and catch him at the commissary node... or search the expanded vessels yourself," offered a passing researcher.

"I suppose," Rollsslowly grumbled as he started swimming briskly along.

He rose against the gravity and nudged against the permeable area. The coral parted, and he slipped out into the current that ran through the center of the vessels used by the human visitors. He drifted with the current, a ridge of appendages raised into the atmosphere to observe the human. He had searched nearly the entire enlarged area before he sensed the taste of a human in the water. He followed the chemical gradient, dropping his appendages to swim more quickly. So he saw the oddly lumpy locomotion appendages that the human used to walk dangling in the water. Rollsslowly felt a flicker of nervousness as he realized that the human's scent glands were giving off stress pheromones. He surfaced and climbed up onto the shelf beside the human.

"What? Rolls?" the human's voice was slurred with nutrient intake, and his skin flushed with stress. He had quickly dropped his hand back behind his center of mass in an odd gesture.

"Are you well, Human Friend Steve?" Rollsslowy asked.

"Well? Sure! Yeah! I'm great!" Human Friend Steve replied. His lips peeled back, revealing his broad, coral-like teeth. The gesture also drew Rollsslowly's attention to the biomatter smeared across the human's lips.

"Very well," Rollsslowly replied. "There is something on your face."

"What?" Human Friend Steve's hand came up from behind him to brush at his face. Rollsslowly noted the object clutched in the human's hands.

"Human Friend Steve," Rollsslowly said in surprise, "I thought you had a negative reaction to foods bearing bovine lactate protein."

Human Friend Steve's eyes twitched, and various shades of irritation and shame washed up and down his face. "I am," he finally said with a long exhale of his lungs.

"Why are you eating something you know will harm you?" Rollsslowly asked in shock.

Human Friend Steve fixed his eyes on Rollsslowly without blinking as defiance flushed across his skin. He deliberately lifted the nutrient solid to his lips, placed it in his mouth, and took a bite. He slowly masticated the nutrients and then swallowed. When he finally replied, his voice was already husky with a buildup of protective mucus.

"Because."

Humans are Weird – The Scent of Heat

"They can smell dangerous heat."

The simple statement carried no context, and Ch'cill curled his secondary legs up underneath him in frustration. Not because he didn't understand Quilx'tch. Far from it. The bizarre situation their expedition had found themselves in provided constant context. 'They' meant the strange biped giants, and no amount of utter grammatical absurdity was cause enough to say that such an utterly ridiculous statement was false.

"I think that you should give me more details, nutritionist," Ch'cill stated calmly.
After the incident with the 'snow' and the nearly miraculous preservation of the exploration team due to the 'warm-blooded' nature of the bipeds, Ch'cill wouldn't directly question Quilx'tch's sanity if he said that a paron beast of legend was politely asking to borrow a cup of nin juice.

"Yes," Quilx'tch visibly shook out his feet as if he was clearing his mind and stiffened to a more rigid posture of attention. "One of the bipeds, the one called Tom, discovered that the third coil on the dorsal ridge of Twitch team's hovercraft was overheating and warned us of the danger."

Ch'cill had never before this expedition wished he was less educated. If he were a happily ignorant brat of some royal family given his position based on his parents' wealth rather than the years of effort he had put in, he might not know how utterly impossible that statement was. He curled his legs again and forced himself to relax and focus on the obvious problem.

"Has the coil been repaired?" Ch'cill asked evenly.

Quilx'tch raised one leg in confirmation. "The technicians saw to that. The biped helped."

"Now," Ch'cill asked patiently, "you say the biped 'smelled dangerous heat'?"

"I don't know how they separated the heat differential from the other temperature differences in the open air!" Quilx'tch said excitedly, scurrying across the room to stand beside the team leader. "But they... he... did! He was just walking past. His eyes weren't even pointed at the craft, and you know how important that is for a binocular vision species! He just stopped, and his head came up – it is so peculiar when they do that, and I think it has *significance* – and he contorted his face and then scouted around until he came to the coils, and he hovered his face over it and asked if it was supposed to be that hot!"

"But how did he know that what he sensed was dangerous?" Ch'cill asked, sorting through the files on his desk. "Tom is listed as a biologist. He is not supposed to have any specialized mechanical knowledge."

"I *know*!" Quilx'tch said happily. "I can't wait to learn more about them. Isn't it fascinating?"

Ch'cill let his abdomen sink to the floor with a tiny sound of distress. It was something... something he was not looking forward to reporting to his superiors.

Humans are Weird – Packing Snow

"Do you hear that?"

Quilx'tch clicked his mandibles in confirmation and adjusted his warming stone underneath his thorax.

"What do you think the humans are up to now?" his younger companion asked, poking her eyes out of her blanket cocoon.

"I don't know," Quilx'tch said, carefully stretching out one leg after another, being careful not to stick his paws out of the 'fleece' the humans had provided him with.

He and his apprentice were sitting facing the data kiosk in the middle of their common room. Both were wrapped closely in the bright red blankets gifted them from the other exploratory species on the planet. The color contrasted with the various dust-colored shelves and containers they held.

"Should we go check on it?" she asked eagerly.

"Do as you wish," Quilx'tch said amiably. "I for one will be waiting here... under my blanket... until the base temperature reaches acceptable levels for the day."

Tas'ka started to shrug off her blanket but shuddered as the air hit her mass and quickly pulled the fleece back over her head. "I can wait," she said.

The odd double beat of approaching human feet heralded the arrival of one of the younger, more eager humans. His bright red face nearly filled their low door as it opened at his signal.

"Hey, Task! Do you want to come out with me?" the human called.

"Out in the cold?" Tas'ka asked.

"Yeah, it snowed last night!" the human said.

"Frozen precipitation has fallen every night for the past forty night cycles," Tas'ka pointed out, adjusting the blanket around her mandibles and eyes.

"Yeah, but this is packing snow!" the human insisted. "First time that has happened."

"I am staying under this lovely blanket until the base reaches optimum temperature," Tas'ka said firmly. "No matter what type of frozen precipitation has fallen."

"Fair enough," the human said with a grin. "I will give you the play by play when we get back in."

The door closed, and the human's footsteps receded.

"Packing snow," Tas'ka mulled over the word. "I wonder what that means…"

"They will tell us," Quilx'tch said, sinking down onto his warming stone with a sigh. "They will no doubt tell us."

Humans are Weird – That is Not a Snake

"It's cool, guys!" Sergeant Grimes waved up at the tree-like plants that now hid two flights of the Winged.

A bright copper head about the size of a golf ball poked out of a cluster of mauve leaves, and twin black eyes glared down at him from under ten horns. "If it is all cool," Twenty-five Clicks demanded, "then why did you just leap half your height into the air and scream out a profanity?"

"There was a cable on the ground," Grimes said, pointing down at the offending item. He bent down and scooped up the length of cable, holding it up for the flights to see. Slowly, more heads popped out of the foliage and glared at the item. Grimes stifled a laugh at the image of a tree full of smol, angry berries.

"Why," Twenty-five Clicks asked as he fluttered down to land on Grime's shoulder, "did you display a fantastic leap… for a human… over a harmless piece of trash?"

"I thought it was a snake," Grimes said with a shrug. He shoved the cable into his backpack as the rest of the flights circled around him.

"That," Twenty-five Clicks said, "looks nothing like the three other items that you claimed triggered this 'snake response.'"

"Does to a human," Grimes replied cheerfully. "And besides, there are lots of snakes. Could look like most any crawly thing."

"Or it is a complicated plot to frighten our species away from this horrific planet full of snakes," a voice muttered from the trees. "An able defense of your homeworld."

"No snakes in the north and south," Grimes corrected as he started walking again.

"You mean the places that are constantly covered in ice," another voice demanded.

"Look," Grimes said with a shrug, "it's a choice. You live where the air hurts your face, or you live where you might get a death bite by a nope-rope at any step."

Twenty-five Clicks bit back a hiss and reminded himself that the human made them safer. He could put up with the strangeness.

Humans are Weird – Human Nonsense

"I really think it is just their pattern-seeking manifesting," Twistunder insisted for the third time.

No one was really satisfied with this answer, least of all him. However, no one in the huddle of Undulates around the datapad argued against the assertion or offered any better explanation. Twistunder ran his best sensory appendage over the screen again just in case he had missed some detail in the image. He hadn't.

"Perhaps we are missing the details due to visual differences?" one of the physiologists suggested. "I mean the meaning might be far simpler than we are assuming."

"Well, that is a given," another pointed out. "All of the charcoal-based iridescence is the same color… or rather lack of color to them."

"Black lines," the first agreed. "It makes it hard to say how much we should read into details that we can see but they cannot."

"Even though they created them," a third said.

The huddle fell silent again. Someone absently stroked Twistunder in a comforting gesture, and he returned it.

"Cuddle puddle," Twistunder muttered.

"Say what?" inquired someone from the bottom of the pile.

"I speculate that this," Twistunder lightly touched one of the more confusing images on the screen, "indicates what we are doing now, a communal huddle. They have labeled it a cuddle puddle."

A hum of thoughtful consideration ran through the huddle as they considered the mass of lines the human had drawn.

"It is the right number of appendages," someone offered, "approximately. If I am seeing this correctly."

"So the question is," Twistunder finally stated, "is this an honest attempt at training material, or is it a joke?"

The huddle fell silent as they examined the primitive visual representations. Twistunder detached himself and mimicked the first entry. Twisting himself into a tight and uncomfortable circle.

"Bagel," one colleague read from the sheet. "Smol fren is lonely. Apply pats."

"Simplistic," Twistunder observed, "but not inaccurate."

"I wouldn't mind a human attempting to physically comfort me if I were in that state honestly," another observed. He curled his appendages under himself and let his notochord relax.

"Unduloaf," his colleague read. "Smol fren is much content but a lil not warmz. Cuddles or to make it warmz suggested."

"Again simplistic," Twistunder began.

"And grammatically nightmarish," a linguist added.

"But accurate as far as it goes," Twistunder finished. "I propose we analyze each image thus. One of us attempts to mimic the drawing, and then we analyze the text."

"And then ask the humans what this nonsense is?" asked the most experienced ambassador.

"And then ask the humans what this nonsense is," Twistunder confirmed.

Humans are Weird – Connotations

"These are some very thorough observations you have taken of the humans' language patterns," First Sister said as she examined the data. "But I fail to comprehend the exact nature of your current research proposal."

Twenty-seventh Cousin flicked her antennae in agreement with the figure on the holo-display. She was all too aware how confusing the mass of data was. "As you are well aware, First Sister," she said, "all known languages have two delineated meanings for each individual idea nodule."

"At least two," First Sister agreed.

"For humanity, this manifests as the connotation or denotation of words," Twenty-seventh Cousin went on, warming to her subject. "Each word has the assigned technical meaning or the denotation, which can be expressed shortly and in writing, and a range of positive and negative associations which require a far greater range of expression to convey."

First Sister spread her antennae in a request for an example.

"'Devour' and 'scarf' for instance have an identical denotation at the current point in time," Twenty-seventh Cousin said. "They converged due to language drift fairly recently. They share the mildly negative connotation of being related to animalistic behavior… however the emotional resonance of 'devour' is frightening and negative while the emotional resonance of 'scarf' is humorous and positive."

First Sister flashed her neck frill in pleased acceptance of the explanation.

"That pair are fairly well understood," Twenty-seventh Cousin went on, "but there is more study to be done in this area. I believe I have found a similarly matched set, but this one is a complex phrase where the denotations are identical, and the connotations are vastly different."

"The far negative reaction being the one you are concerned about the Core University Institutional Review Board rejecting the study for," First Sister said, one antenna bobbing slowly in understanding.

Twenty-seventh Cousin flared her frill in relief and confirmation.

"And you want me to aid you in formulating the study so it isn't rejected," First Sister went on thoughtfully.

Twenty-seventh Cousin tried to keep her antennae from twitching in excited anticipation like a newly emerged.

"I am afraid I can't," First Sister said with a very disappointed droop of her frill.

Twenty-seventh Cousin tried not to twitch in irritation. She well knew the first of her hive, and First Sister had no intention of disappointing her younger hivemate. However, there was some mischief twitching at the end of her mandibles, and Twenty-seventh Cousin knew better than to attempt to force the issue.

"I am disappointed," she said tonelessly, playing along. "What am I to do?"

"Well," First Sister brushed back her antennae dramatically, "the duties of a newly mated are so many, but I suppose—"

"The duties of a what?" Twenty-seventh Cousin's frill snapped out to full and washed green with blood flow; her antennae positively danced, and she even lost professional control of her voice, letting it shoot out of the common range into the native trill of her species.

First Sister clicked in mock surprise and flicked her mandibles to the side like an old matron. "Weren't you told, dear one?" she asked in a calm and professional tone. Only the rapid fluttering of her frill behind her neck gave her excitement away.

Twenty-seventh Cousin laid her antennae back in an emphatic negative.

"Well," First Sister shook herself and gestured off screen. "As I was saying, I cannot attend to this at the moment... but Second Brother here."

An absolutely gorgeous male stepped into frame with her. He was a smooth, creamy green all over with a brilliant red semi-frill around his neck coming to a point just over his thorax. His antennae were long and amazingly flexible, coming nearly to First Sister's neck when alert with interest. His eyes were the color of amber with facets so well-defined that the Crystals of the Mother would have wept for envy. They were wide-set as well. A human might have splayed out their hand full width to pat his head and not touched either eye with pinky or thumb. His mandibles positively gleamed with health when they moved. Which they were doing now.

Twenty-seventh Cousin started up and laid her antennae back in shame.

"Forgive me," she said hurriedly. "I didn't hear that. I was somewhat... surprised by the sudden—"

"So we saw," First Sister said in a smug tone. "What my dear Second Brother was saying was that he would be glad to come personally and assist you with your study. He is a very proficient linguist and specializes in human – oh, what is that strange organ term they use?"

"Tongues," Second Brother offered with a shy flick of his supple antennae.

Twenty-seventh Cousin didn't know if a frill could actually burst from pride, but First Sister looked to be in severe danger of it.

"I would be glad to have his assistance," Twenty-seventh Cousin said with full sincerity. Antennae-paralyzing beauty aside, a University-trained linguist would be just what she needed. "But how can you spare him?" she asked.

"Given the cycle, we won't be stringing any lines in the garden for some time," First Sister said with a dismissive flick of her antennae.

Second Brother ducked his head in embarrassment at the blunt statement, but his antennae were twitching with delight. First Sister nudged him pointedly with a foot joint.

"I really do think the time would be better spent getting to know the rest of the hive," he said softly, "before I have too much responsibility to wander."

Great Mother, he has a voice like wind chimes, Twenty-seventh Cousin thought.

"That would be ideal," she said. She forcibly refocused her attention away from her new cousin and indicated the data. He leaned forward eagerly and read through it. He soon clicked in understanding.

"You will most likely want someone non-threatening to ask the questions," he said. "I can do that."

She clicked gratefully. "That would be wonderful," she said. "For some reason all the humans on this base are nervous around me."

"Curious," Second Brother said without taking his attention off of the data. "You have such a charming mandible set."

"Be that as it may," she replied, "I think you will be a far better non-threatening questioner."

"So the concept is," he said as he finished the data, "is that I am to come up to individual humans while they are isolated, ask them one of two nearly identical questions, and record their emotive responses?"

Twenty-seventh Cousin flicked her antennae in confirmation.

Second Brother clicked a few times as he prepared to use human speech. Then straightened and spoke. "Human Friend, would you like to accompany me to my cottage in the forest?" he tried the first question. "Human Friend, would you like to accompany me to my cabin in the woods?" He had an excellent grasp of the human language, and both sentences were smooth. "And you say that the first one is met with general positivity and the second with general fear and hostility?" he asked.

"It is more than that," Twenty-seventh Cousin explained. "I showed the question set to a human, and he assured me the connotation set was pleasant and vague for the first but very specifically being hacked to death by an insane human after a prolonged pursuit for the second."

Second Brother curled his antennae in horror. "That is very specific for connotation," he observed. "What could have caused that?"

Humans are Weird – Pardon Me

"Pardon me, Human Friend LaChance?" Twistunder began as he approached the human at the edge of the joint recreation pool.

"Eh?"

The sound was listed as *general recognition of non-threatening disturbance – continue to communicate – repeat previous communication attempt.* It was quite a lot of meaning to imprint in one tone, and Twistunder was rather fascinated with the idea, but he was here for a different and potentially more offensive set of questions.

"Pardon me, Human Friend LaChance," Twistunder began again. "May I intrude on your meditation time?"

"My what now?" LaChance asked, his face twisting into perplexed and relaxed confusion.

"You are reading and meditating over the thoughts in that book," Twistunder indicated the woven mass of rustling lanolin.

"Yeah," the human said as he examined the book, and his face smoothed over in surprise, his stripes flushing alternating colors. "I guess that is what I am doing… what was your question?"

"I asked," Twistunder repeated, "if I may intrude."

"Intrude away, little buddy," Human Friend LaChance said cheerfully.

Taking that as a full invitation, Twistunder quickly scrambled out of the water onto the rock the human was sitting on and up into the twin broad mobile appendages. Twistunder marveled anew at the tightly bound masses of muscle under the thick and rough outer membrane. It was easy to believe that a human could race across the ground at a fantastic six unds per second. Human Friend LaChance let out a rumble from deep in his chest that was called a chuckle as Twistunder settled over his primary appendage joints.

"I have a question," Twistunder began, making sure to angle his primary gripping end at Human Friend LaChance's face. "It is a question that might be offensive."

"We're both scientists," LaChance replied, twisting his face to reveal his broad, enameled teeth. "I doubt I'll be offended."

"I wish to ask the meaning of that physical word you just used," Twistunder replied.

"I used a physical word?" Human Friend LaChance asked in surprise.

"Yes," Twistunder explained.

"So what made you think it was maybe offensive?" Human Friend LaChance asked.

"It was very similar to the poem prayer," Twistunder answered, displaying the motion with one appendage.

"Well, not offended but then again very much not Catholic," Human Friend LaChance said with a laugh. "And I certainly wasn't praying just now… physically or otherwise. Can you show me what I did?"

Twistunder bobbed his primary gripping end eagerly up and down in confirmation.

"You did this," he said. He arched his body up, gripping Human Friend LaChance's kneecaps for support, and stiffened into his best approximation of a bipedal form. He lifted one primary gripping appendage and lightly tapped first the top of his 'head,' then his 'face,' then his 'chest.' Human Friend LaChance burst out laughing so hard that Twistunder had to drop back down and grip both legs to avoid falling off. When the laughter subsided, Human Friend LaChance reached down to pat him in a friendly gesture.

"Not meant to be communication, bud," he said cheerfully. "It is more of an internal reaction to circumstances." Twistunder drooped in disappointment, and Human Friend LaChance patted him again. "But I can translate it for you as communication anyway," Human Friend LaChance assured him.

He stiffened in the first gesture.

"Hey! I need my glasses!" he said. "You know what glasses are, right?"

"Artificial light focal point generators made from various crystalline substances," Twistunder replied.

"Yup! So then," he touched the top of his head, "are they on my head? No? Well, maybe I already put them on my eyes and just forgot." He touched the wide bones over his eyes. "Nope? Well, maybe I hung them on my neck?" He touched his chest. "Nope. Guess I left them at home. No biggie." The human ceased the explanation and smiled down at his friend as he patted him. "That explain it for you, bud?" he asked.

"It is an external diagnostic," Twistunder observed.

"Pretty much," Human Friend LaChance said with a shrug.

"Thank you, Human Friend LaChance," Twistunder said.

The Undulate settled down on the human's legs as LaChance leaned back and resumed reading. Writing up reports about human behavior was fine and all, but sunning on top of a warm mammalian muscle mass was something worth doing too.

Humans are Weird – Not Hiding

"Why are we hiding, Human Friend Steve?" Thrustup asked from where he poised on the shelf over the human.

Human Friend Steve started with a profanity and jerked away from the wall he had been pressed against. "I'm not hiding!" Human Friend Steve insisted, his striped skin flushing brilliant colors in turn as the blood flow altered.

"Really?" Thrustup asked. "I thought that posture and your relationship to the local environments indicated an attempt at concealment. I will have to—"

"Maybe I was hiding a little," Human Friend Steve admitted, rubbing his primary gripping appendage over his face, sending the colorful stripes there rippling. "I didn't mean to be hiding. It was just —"

"An instinctive reaction to some threat?" Thrustup asked, his voice going flat as unease made him lose control of his ability to generate sound.

"Not a threat," Human Friend Steve said with a resigned sigh. The human angled his core mass so his sensory concentration, his 'head,' was aimed around the corner. "Just avoiding another human," Human Friend Steve confessed.

"Is there a dispute between you?" Thrustup asked, adding concern to his voice.

"No, no," Human Friend Steve said, adding with a gesture of his primary gripping appendage that the idea was so far from the truth that it ought to be dismissed and not brought up again. "We're fine. Really. It's just I was up a little late last night, and I don't want to be stuck next to that chatterbox till the coffee kicks in."

"Chatterbox?" Twistunder asked after a pause.

"Human Friend Madeline," Human Friend Steve explained. "She talks a lot, and she has a kind of high-pitched voice. It doesn't bother me when I'm properly rested, but when I'm still groggy…" he waved his gripping appendage in a gesture of generic confirmation.

Thrustup considered this. "Why are you hiding then?" he asked.

"I'm not hiding!" Human Friend Steve protested again. "Not really. I just don't want to hurt Maddie's feelings, so I'm waiting to go for the coffee pot until she goes out to the gardens."

"How would you hurt her feelings?" Thrustup asked.

"By refusing to listen to what she is saying," Human Friend Steve explained as he peered around the corner again.

"Will not your hiding from her over here hurt her feelings in the same way?" Thrustup asked.

"She won't know about it if people keep quiet," Human Friend Steve muttered.

"Do you wish me to stop talking?" Thrustup asked. "Or I can lower the pitch of my voice."

Human Friend Steve loosened and let the broad, bony surface of his head slap into the wall. "I need coffee for this conversation," he groaned.

Humans are Weird – Leaf Them Alone

It wasn't every day one was called before the ethics in sentience research committee. It certainly had never happened to Feeling the Joy of Generosity. Even so, he was strongly aware that he was in the absolute surface of disgrace. If they didn't want to drag him up to the surface to wither, he didn't know anything about animal sentience.

"And it is kind of my job to know things about animal sentience," he released a long sigh of gas and shuffled his feet (he was proud of those feet) along the floor of the too-sterile building.

Feeling the Joy of Generosity could feel the pulsing of the electrical systems in the walls, and his tendrils twitched longingly. However, nothing was quite so alluring as the steady rush and flow of the nutrient rich water that flowed through the pipes though. He wondered if it were really such a good thing that the other species treated it with such harsh minerals. Surely the danger of an overwhelming outgrowth wasn't that bad?

An Undulate passed by him, the water in its transport tank sloshing invitingly. Before he could think better of it, Feeling the Joy of Generosity raised a hand and dropped it into the tank. The Undulate let out a disgusted blurp and shimmied out of the tank as fast as he could. Feeling the Joy of Generosity's hand dissolved in the water, and he pulled back his neural tendrils with another sigh.

"My apologies, Friend Undulate," he said in the human language. He thought most Undulates had learned the human vibration language. This one however simply shuffled off down the hall, abandoning the now contaminated transport tank. Feeling the Joy of Generosity reached in with another hand to try and remove the solid material only to have the second hand dissolve as well. Giving up the

240

attempt to reclaim his duff matter, he coiled all his exposed tendrils in and shuffled down the hall towards the room where the committee waited. The door swished open at his approach, dislodging quite a bit of his head covering. Feeling the Joy of Generosity pulled those tendrils back in as well and tried not to think of it as a bad omen.

A Shatar sat at the head of the table, and a small, elderly flight of Winged hung from perches on the ceiling. The Undulate representative had abandoned her comfort tank to drape herself across the human representative's shoulders. A ramp had been formed into the table leading to a concave depression in the center. Feeling the Joy of Generosity centered his minerals and shuffled up to the depression. He relaxed into it. He carefully formed a pair of bright yellow eyes to point at each of the representatives. The animals all squirmed uncomfortably until he had settled his form.

"Feeling the Joy of Generosity," the Shatar began, her neck frill spreading out in a stern display of her colors, "do you know why we called you here?"

"I suspect so," Feeling the Joy of Generosity replied, making sure that his outer duff layer was showing proper colors of submission to the Shatar.

"Good," the Shatar said. "Now, is it true that you performed scientific experiments on humans without their knowledge or consent?"

Feeling the Joy of Generosity squirmed uneasily. "I really didn't mean to," he offered. "It just sort of… happened."

The Shatar laid back her frill and focused her faceted eyes on him in a long, searching look. The human was chuckling and petting the agitated Undulate soothingly.

"How in the name of the First Flight do you accidentally perform a scientific experiment on a sentient being of that mass?" demanded the leader of the Winged Flight.

"Well, it started last fall," Feeling the Joy of Generosity began. "I noticed an odd behavior in the humans on the base. I got curious and kept watching. Then I changed a few variables. Then I took notes so I wouldn't lose the data in walking. Before I knew it, I had a case study going."

"What was the behavior you noted?" the Undulate asked.

"Well," Feeling the Joy of Generosity began, "they were stepping on my leafs."

"Human feet are three times the size of any one of us," a Winged pointed out. "They can hardly avoid stepping on everything."

"Ah, yes," Feeling the Joy of Generosity agreed. "But they were going out of their way to step on particular leafs."

"Begin at the beginning," the Shatar ordered him with a wave of her hand.

"I was out sunning," Feeling the Joy of Generosity said. "I wanted to catch the last warm afternoon radiance of the year before the snows came. You know if we don't do that, we can go deep dormant over winter and lose decades of life."

"You were sunning," the Shatar noted coolly.

"Now the cold and the sun had dried out a lot of my leafs," Feeling the Joy of Generosity went on. "Most of them I managed to absorb into my main tendril mass, but there were a lot that were just way too large and tough for me to digest over winter, so I just drained them and let them blow off."

"You are aware that we do not allow the shedding of sentient exposed biomatter without proper precautions," the Shatar pointed out.

"I am now," he admitted.

"Continue," the Shatar ordered.

"Well, I was sunning there. I was kind of lonely," he went on. "When one of the human mechanics approached. I wanted to talk to him, but I really needed that sun, so I just watched him walk past. Then the wind picked up some of my rejected leafs and sent them skittering across the ground. One landed in front of the human, and he broke stride to step on it. He grinned." Feeling the Joy of Generosity paused and mulled over his next statement. "He really enjoyed it. I think," he said. "Anyway, he saw another leaf and changed his course to step on it too, but then he just went on his way."

"There were other desiccated leafs remaining?" the Undulate asked, interested now.

"We are investigating Feeling the Joy of Generosity's actions here," the Shatar reminded them, "not human behavior."

"There were other leafs," Feeling the Joy of Generosity replied. "He did ignore them. I observed this behavior in other base humans too. I had nothing else to do while I composted for winter, so I started making the crisp leafs purposely and leaving them in various locations. Then winter came." He shuddered at the memory of the weeks trapped under the icy blanket that blocked out the sun and drove all the other species into their sterile structures. "I composted on it all winter," he explained, "and when spring came, I simply continued what I had been doing but took notes on the behavior."

"So the only thing you really did," the human finally inquired, "was drop your leafs deliberately instead of randomly?"

"And took notes," Feeling the Joy of Generosity reminded him.

The human laughed, and the Shatar flared her frill at the mammal in annoyance.

"So what did you discover?" the human asked, ignoring the Shatar.

"That most humans will consistently deviate from their path to compress a desiccated leaf," Feeling the Joy of Generosity stated. "But only for desiccated leafs and only for leafs within a few feet of their pre-designated path."

"I will go slightly out of my way to step on that crunchy leaf," the human murmured in a delighted tone.

"What?" the Undulate asked in confusion.

"What?" the human asked with a look of mock innocence.

Humans are Weird – Itchy

"There is something wrong with one of the humans," Grind announced as he shuffled into the base commander's office.

Twenty-fifth Trill sighed and peered over the edge of his work station to glare down at Grind. It was pricking at the tips of his sensory horns to suggest that there was something not quite right about the base medic himself, but he restrained himself. The Gathering was a pale gray that was considered an unhealthy tint by every other species he knew of, but as there was no medical condition listed on Grind's file, he could only assume that the pallor was a normal morph for the reptilian species.

"I take it you mean something other than the usual human brand of near suicidal lack of self-awareness?" Twenty-fifth Trill said instead.

Grind paused in the stiff shuffle that served his species as locomotion and dangled his broad, scaled head up at Twenty-fifth Trill. One of his yellow eyes focused on the Winged, and he slowly blinked.

"Yes," he finally growled through his conical teeth.

Twenty-fifth Trill heaved a sigh and fluttered down with his portable input device. "Permission to land?" he asked. He did try not to be stiff about it. The humans on the base never required permission to land on their broad, flat surfaces. The Shatar did of course, but that was natural; most of their ideal landing areas were actually highly sensitive sensory organs. The Gathering had almost as much sensor-dull surface area as humans despite being less than a third their size, but they were so twitching about sharing it. Despite it being armored even.

BETTY ADAMS

"Wherever you like," grunted out the base medic.

Twenty-fifth Trill took him at his word and landed directly between his wide-set eyes. Both turned in to glare at him, and Twenty-fifth Trill smiled cheerfully back at him. He was ever grateful he'd taken the time to learn that gesture from the humans in University.

"He has a skin irritation," Grind finally said, apparently deciding to forgo their favorite argument for the moment in favor of work.

"And I take it he won't come to you with the issue?" Twenty-fifth Trill asked.

"No," Grind replied.

"And how did you discover this complaint?" Twenty-fifth Trill asked.

"He was scratching his back on the doorjamb," Grind explained.

Twenty-fifth Trill felt his outer ears perk in interest. "Really now?" he asked.

"Don't misunderstand," Grind snapped. "His feet are firmly on the ground. Very firmly. I mean that he is using the ninety degree angle of the doorjamb as a surface to vigorously rub his back against in a sideways motion."

"Ah!" Twenty-fifth Trill slumped in disappointment as visions of the human clinging to the walls like a normal person faded away. "To reach the unscratchable itch."

"You've heard of this behavior?" Grind asked.

"Yes," Twenty-fifth Trill replied. "It is fairly common. Probably psychological in origin. You have heard of the 'big red button' phenomenon?"

247

Grind gave a curt nod that nearly unseated Twenty-fifth Trill.

"Well, the reality of their massive limb bones means there is usually one spot on their backs that they can't scratch on their own," Twenty-fifth Trill went on. "It often becomes inflamed with psychosomatic itching. The psychs think the purpose is to drive them to seek communal grooming contact."

Grind looked unconvinced.

"Just offer to scratch his back instead of phrasing it as a suggestion to come in for a medical evaluation," Twenty-fifth Trill suggested. "He will be more likely to agree, and you can get a diagnosis on the sly if you suspect it's more than just the usual human weirdness."

Humans are Weird – Procrastination

"Human Friend Pyre?" Fourth Sister asked. "Do you have the files on the graminoids moisture flow prepared?"

The human turned away from his computer screen and squinted up at her. The twin slits glinted up at her and sent a shiver through her frill. Sapient predator species were still a new concept to the galaxy at large, and she certainly wasn't quite sure how to take the knowledge they existed.

"What'cha need, Sis?" Human Friend Pyre asked.

"The files on the graminoids you were writing," Fourth Sister repeated.

"Yeah, that," Human Friend Pyre said. His head bobbed, and he began flexing his fleshy digits around what he had told her was a stress ball. "Thought those weren't due till tomorrow," he observed.

"They are not," Fourth Sister confirmed. "However, with the delay in the supply shipment, we have all had a decrease in our workload, and I thought you might have used this time to finish the project you are currently working on. Did something of a higher priority come up?"

"Nah," Human Friend Pyre waved away the idea. "I'm just procrastinating is all. It'll be done by the time it's due."

"Very well," Fourth Sister said, unsure how to end the interaction. "I will communicate with you after the due date has been reached."

Human Friend Pyre grunted and returned his attention to his screen. Fourth Sister turned slowly away and pondered if this was anything she could bring to their supervisor's attention.

Humans are Weird – Only if it Can Catch Me

"Hey, mate! Look what I found under that rock! Isn't it awesome!"

Quilx'tch leapt back from the writhing mass of scales, impossibly tiny (and razor sharp) talons, and apparently pure hate that the human was holding out to him with a wide smile.

"Human Friend Tom," Quilx'tch said, hoping that he had mastered the tones to project firmness to the human. "Is that dangerous?"

"Naw! Not a bit!" the human scoffed.

"I mean is it dangerous to me?" Quilx'tch clarified. "Or anyone of my approximate size?" *And my lack of insanity*, Quilx'tch thought privately. He could see the thought process going on behind the human's two giant eyes as Tom looked back and forth between the toothy horror in his hands and the nutritionist. A frown creased his face. *That means he is either thinking about this for the first time or is discomforted*, mused Quilx'tch idly.

"Well, I don't think so," Tom said slowly. "I mean… it is pretty slow. You should be able to outrun it easy enough."

"So your definition of dangerous," Quilx'tch said, "is that it can't kill you if it can't catch you?"

"Yup!" Tom nodded eagerly and thrust the horror forward again. "Ain't she beautiful?"

Humans are Weird – Pâté

"Hey, little buddy!" Human Friend Mick called out to Quilx'tch as he entered the commissary on the raised walkway.

Deciding that the gregarious Mick was as good a place to start as anywhere, Quilx'tch scampered over to him across the raised walkways the humans called the spiderwalks. Quilx'tch estimated the mounds of biomass still left on Human Friend Mick's plate and decided that he planned to be here for a while longer.

"You got your thinking pad out, little buddy," Human Friend Mick observed, waving a spoon at the datapad Quilx'tch held. "You got more food questions?"

"That I do, Human Friend Mick," Quilx'tch replied. "Would you—"

"Ask away, ask away," Human Friend Mick interrupted with a cheerful grin. "Always glad to make the life of our resident nutritional anthropologist a little easier."

Quilx'tch twitched at the rudeness of the interruption but had no trouble suppressing the reaction below the human's perception threshold. He had interacted with the Winged for long enough that human jollity did little to disturb him.

"Would you answer some questions about human proclivity for nutrient specific eating patterns?" Quilx'tch continued.

"Sure," Human Friend Mick replied. "As long as you use smaller words."

"You are currently eating?" Quilx'tch asked, raising a primary gripping appendage to indicate the spoon that was going back and forth between the human's dish and mouth.

"Vanilla pudding!" Human Friend Mick said eagerly.

"And it is customary to eat it in such a way?" Quilx'tch asked.

"With a spoon from a cup?" Human Friend Mick asked. "Yeah, I guess sometimes we put it in other food as an ingredient, but we eat it like this mostly."

"Do you eat frosting in that manner?" Quilx'tch asked.

Human Friend Mick stared at him blankly for a moment as the massive brain behind the strangely complex and beautiful eyes worked on the answer.

"No," he finally said slowly. "You'd never eat frosting from a cup. I mean… you might snatch a little as you were putting it on a cake or something like that, but no."

"Why not?" Quilx'tch asked. "The nutrient profile is very similar."

"I…" Human Friend Mick stared at him blankly for enough time that Quilx'tch nearly laughed at how the confusion neatly mimicked proper Trisk politeness. "I don't know. I just don't know."

"Very well," Quilx'tch said as he noted the answer. "Do you eat chowder in this manner?"

"Pretty much," Human Friend Mick said with a shake of his body as if he were clearing sleep dust from his exoskeleton. "But we heat it first."

"Do you eat mayonnaise in this manner?" Quilx'tch asked.

Human Friend Mick stared at him for quite a long span this time, and his face tightened in thought as he gathered to the point of this survey. That pattern recognition was what made gathering data on them so frustrating. The 'n' had to be massive for any data to be relevant. Which was why he was here.

"No," Human Friend Mick finally said. "Never."

"Refried beans?" Quilx'tch asked.

"Yes," Human Friend Mick replied.

"Peanut butter?"

"No."

"Salsa?"

"No."

"Fruit salad?"

"Yes."

"Smoothies?"

"Yes."

"Ketchup?"

"No."

"Mustard?"

"No."

"Miso?"

"Yes."

"Yogurt?"

"Yes."

"Milkshakes?"

"Double yes."

"Tartar sauce?"

"Double no!"

"Pâté?"

"No again."

"Strained beets?"

"Mostly not, but some folks really like 'em."

Quilx'tch stared down at the data and idly tapped his pad in thought.

"Is that all the questions?" Human Friend Mick interrupted his musing.

"Oh, I have many more questions," Quilx'tch replied, "but no more for this particular survey. Thank you for your aid, Human Friend Mick."

"No problem, little buddy," Human Friend Mick replied cheerfully.

Quilx'tch made the courteous goodbyes and leapt back up to the spiderwalks. Before he left the room, he heard Human Friend Mick mutter, "Why don't we eat frosting with a spoon?"

Humans are Weird – A Vague Memory

Shiftssubtly had never been the keenest of observers. Oh, don't get him wrong; in his own field he could tell if a bolt was a hundredth of an und off of perfect torque. But when it came to non-mechanical things, well, he was a very good mechanic. This lack of observational skill had led to several write-ups, confabs with base commanders, and the occasional punting. For despite his near complete interpersonal blindness, he really, truly enjoyed human company. But apparently there were all these subtle rules that he simply could not fathom.

Humans loved to share body warmth. But a tenth of an und to the wrong in any direction might get your lap cuddling privileges revoked. The entire width and breadth of the 'back' region was available for lounging if the human was prone. But get too far – and how far was too far varied for each human – from the cage of structural integrity supports, and the human might start spasming. It was just all too complicated. On all the other appendages, a single lazy day spent lounging in all that radiated warmth with the softly glowing strips on full display under your appendages was worth nearly any amount of trouble.

So when Shiftssubtly swam into the shared dining area and saw Human Friend Bobby slumped in the corner, it occurred to him that this might be a good time to nurture some goodwill growth. Shiftssubtly browsed through the various algae gardens provided and deliberately chose the stringiest variety. Ones he could easily transport. He wound them around his secondary appendages and swam towards where Human Friend Bobby still slumped in the corner. The plasiglass ceiling of the swimming tunnels rang with the rhythmic, quadruple pounding of the motile humans' steps. Shiftssubtly came up under Human Friend Bobby's table and climbed up the chair, using that added height to boost himself onto the table surface.

He hummed in contentment. Human Friend Bobby had not recognized him and was staring off into the distance, his lower mandible resting in the cradle of the only ten truly functional appendages the humans had. Shiftssubtly had been correct then. Human Friend Bobby was distressed over something. While Shiftssubtly would freely admit that he might be misinterpreting the human's body language, the fact that the human was softly chanting the universal profanity was a fairly calcified indicator.

"Human Friend Bobby," Shiftssubtly began.

The human started and clutched his appendages to the ventral region of his body. "Ey, Shifty!" the human said with a gasp. "Didn't see you swim up."

"Very understandable with your limited visual range," Shiftssubtly agreed. "It is what makes you vulnerable to predators, correct?"

Human Friend Bobby stared at him for a moment, his face going slack in what Shiftssubtly took to indicate deep thinking. "I guess?" Human Friend Bobby finally replied.

Shiftssubtly arranged the algae strands so that fresh surface area was touching his absorptive areas. "Would it be impolite for me to ask what is causing you emotional distress?" Shiftssubtly asked.

He was about to go on and suggest digestive distress. He was told it was very common among species with internal digestive organs, but he remembered at the last moment that humans didn't always like talking about their internal organs. However, before he could reformulate the question, Human Friend Bobby vented a massive gust of atmosphere and dramatically rearranged his pectoral appendages into a tripod and oscillated his caudal end. Shiftssubtly took that as a negative and was about to change the subject when the human spoke.

"I just don't know, Shifty," Human Friend Bobby said. "You see it's like this. I think I agreed to do something last night." The human paused and freed five of his appendages to prod at the lump of semi-processed protein on his plate.

"Do you object to doing the thing?" Shiftssubtly asked.

"I don't even know what the thing is!" Human Friend Bobby exclaimed, tossing his caudal end back suddenly and running all ten functional appendages through his fibrous caudal covering.

"They why did you agree to it?" Shiftssubtly asked.

"It was late," Human Friend Bobby said, "like real late. Two this morning, I think. My comm buzzed and woke me up. Sort of. I think. And so two A.M. me looked at my phone, and someone requested I do something, so two A.M. me says sure, fine, whatever, and goes back to sleep. And now I can't remember who it was or what they asked me to do, but I totally agreed to do it. So now I either flake out on someone or go around the base like an idiot first-year cadet asking what I agreed to last night."

The human slumped back down and resumed prodding at his nutrient lump. Shiftssubtly took a moment to work over his options and, deciding that he had no solution to offer the human, reached out and patted the broad surface where all the useful appendages attached.

"I am sure you will work out a successful solution," Shiftssubtly assured him. "And if you cannot, remember the base is mostly Undulates, and we are very hard to offend."

The human smiled weakly at him, and the stripes on his face began to pulse with renewed life. "Thanks, Shifty," Human Friend Bobby said. "You're a real pal."

Elated at his success, Shiftssubtly pushed on. "Besides," he said, drawing on a bit of human philosophy he had once overheard, "no one will remember it when you die in a few decades."

Assuming his work here was done successfully, the Undulate slipped back over the edge of the table and into the tunnel entrance with a splash. He idly noted that Human Friend Bobby had followed the motion with his eyes and was watching him with an oddly intent expression. Shiftssubtly waved a farewell appendage and mulled over the revelation the human had made. If the humans did indeed have two separate personalities, a night and day personality as it were, that might explain why he had such trouble interacting with them. He should probably bring this up to the base commander.

Humans are Weird – 100 Strokes

"Fourth Accountant, Seventh Administrative Aide," Twenty-second Sister dipped her antennae to each of the humans in turn as she approached them.

The human sitting and working the terrifying device glanced at her and nodded politely with her hands, not skipping a single stroke. The human who was the focus of this behavior waved a hand in Twenty-second Sister's general direction in a languid manner.

"Sup, Sis?" the reclining human asked, her voice thick with contentment and relaxation.

Twenty-second Sister fought down a confused flutter of her frill. She was here to figure out this mystery. Fourth Accountant kept her fibrous radiation shield cropped short to the point of being almost useless for its designated purpose. Seventh Administrative Aide kept her radiation shield at the maximum length allowed by her genetics. Usually it was kept back in a neat braid that gave it the appearance of some antennae/frill hybrid that wasn't entirely unaesthetic to the Shatar. At the moment, Seventh Administrative Aide had loosened the strands and held the restraining bands around her wrist. Fourth Accountant was dragging a paddle covered in rigid bristles through the fibers in a way that made Twenty-second Sister's antennae twitch with sympathetic pain.

"I had a question," Twenty-second Sister began carefully. "A cultural question."

"Fire away!" Seventh Administrative Aide said with another wave of her hands.

"What is the purpose of this social interaction?" Twenty-second Sister asked, indicating what they were doing with her antennae.

"Social bonding through mutual grooming of course," Fourth Accountant said brightly.

"Yes," Twenty-second Sister curled her antennae in understanding. "But what actual physical benefit does grooming give? You cannot be removing mites…"

Both humans laughed at that.

"What benefit does it give?" Seventh Administrative Aide asked. "I just do it because Grandma taught me to. One hundred strokes every night and all that?"

"It distributes the oil from your scalp glands," Fourth Accountant explained. "I just get a caustic enough soap and get the oil out that way every day, but since you have to worry about keeping your hair from splitting at the ends too fast, you need your oil. Does that explain it, Sis?"

They glanced at her, Seventh Administrative Aide even peeling open one eye to look at her. Twenty-second Sister stood in shocked amazement.

"You have glands," she began slowly, "that simply pump lipids out of your body that actually excrete them from your outer membrane? You are… constantly leaking?"

"I guess," Fourth Accountant said with a shrug. "Helps keep the mites at bay, I suppose."

"I… thank you," Twenty-second Sister said as she beat a hasty retreat from the steady swishing of the bristled paddle and the suddenly greasy humans.

Humans are Weird – Domestication

"And the woman braided her hair once more, and the dog became the First Friend," the human concluded.

The fire crackled merrily for a moment in camp, the only other sound the rippling of the small pond. A pair of amber appendages reached out of the water and nudged a log further into the fire.

"That was a very interesting story," the breadbox-sized alien said, its voice flattened by fatigue and filtering through the water. "Are there other stories about domesticating animals?"

"Oh, tons," Mack Dodge said with a yawn. "But I should probably mention that 'Just So Stories' aren't proper legends."

"How can a legend be not proper?" Twistunder asked.

"Oh, a proper legend started so long ago that no one remembers when or how it started, I suppose," Mack explained. "We know exactly when this one started and who wrote it and why."

"I see," Twistunder said. "What about your domestic plants?"

"Hmm," Mack mused aloud. "I can't think of any stories off the top of my head. I know some quotes about domestic roses though. We domesticated them so long ago no one knows when, so it is sort of legendary."

"Roses?" Twistunder asked.

"Big, flowering structure on a plant we bred to have dozens more sepals than the wildtype," Mack said, waving his hand. "Forms shrub structures, nasty thorns. Symbolizes various types of love and affection. Got a scar from one on my arm." Mack pointed to a thin, white line on his forearm.

"Why were you handling the wildtype?" Twistunder asked as Mack's tired voice drifted off.

"Huh?" Mack asked. "Nah, the wildtype roses don't have serious thorns. I mean not bad enough to tear skin like that. It's the domestic ones that got the really big thorns."

The night descended into quiet again until Twistunder raised his voice again.

"Do you mean to tell me that your ancient ancestors deliberately weaponized an ornamental flowering plant? And decided that this was to be the symbol for all the various types of love and affection?"

"I guess so," Mack said with a yawn. "Night, Twist."

Twistunder grumbled softly to himself as he reached for his tablet. Why did humans so consistently drop paradigm-changing facts on him right before he needed to go to sleep?

Humans are Weird – Something You Don't Believe In

"Well, everything was fine until the screaming started," Reactsslowly explained as he lifted his remaining gripping appendage in what the investigating officer assumed was supposed to be half of an explanatory gesture.

Tightensgrimly laced his gripping appendages together and swelled his main mass above it in a threatening gesture. The small space of the comfortably darkened meeting room seemed to amplify the gesture. The younger Undulate went limp in response, and the investigator raised one gripping appendage meaningfully.

"Start from the gripping end," Reactsslowly said, releasing a wash of submissive pheromones. "Right."

Tightensgrimly waved for the injured Undulate to continue.

"As you are aware, the tides on this world are extra strong," Reactsslowly began. "We were all briefed on that when we got here. It gets cold too; too cold to be out there alone for very long. It's not as bad as the death world. I mean the humans consider it a prime world, but it gets cold enough to slow you down, and I'm clearly not all that fast to begin with."

Reactsslowly wriggled his newly regenerating stumps in demonstration, and Tightensgrimly waved for him to continue.

"So we were all briefed on these two factors, and the humans were briefed on it too because they can get hypothermic too. Even with that massive metabolism of theirs, they can only stay out so long, way longer than us of course, but still they understand, you know?"

Tightensgrimly flicked a lagging appendage in agreement. He did know.

"So I was assigned to this base and got the training and made friends with the human on my shift like we're supposed to, you know? Expand cross-species awareness."

Reactsslowly was rolling into his story now, and Tightensgrimly settled back to take notes.

"Human Friend Bob was really friendly and curious. He asked about everything, even about regeneration, which was weird, looking back up the roll, you know? Because he knew. I explained it to him really good. But he was still, well, you've seen the recordings and heard them." Reactsslowly paused to shudder at the memory. "Anyway, I had the training, and Bob had the training, and we went out a lot to gather algae samples together a lot. You know, that red-green hybrid that comes from Earth that we can eat too? Not very high protein but really cold tolerant, so we think that if we can get it to the colonies on…"

Reactsslowly let that tangle of thought die as Tightensgrimly began to spread with irritation again.

"So we went out this one day," Reactsslowly began again. "Only there were storm waves moving in. You know what storm waves are?"

Tightensgrimly flicked an appendage in assent and didn't scold the younger Undulate. It was a legitimate question. The phenomenon was nearly unheard of on their home world.

"So Bob was scoffing at the storm waves. He called them barely breakers, and we were out most of the morning installing the protective gates that snap shut on the waves. You know the gates that keep the algae from getting too agitated while letting them get plenty of movement? So we installed those, and then Bob got called back to the main base to help with some heavy lifting, and I stayed out to finish

HUMANS ARE WEIRD: I HAVE THE DATA

the installation. It took me pretty long being alone, and the waves had moved in by the time I was done. The sun was going down, and I was getting a little cold and slow."

Tightensgrimly pointedly raised a gripping appendage.

"Yes, yes," Reactsslowly said with a sigh. "I know that will be on my report. I just wanted to get the job done so badly. If the waves moved in, we would lose nearly half a year's growth on the hybrid."

Tightensgrimly swelled with fury.

"But it wasn't worth my safety," Reactsslowly quickly interjected. "Bad me. I'll do better next time."

Tightensgrimly twisted a look of skepticism at the other Undulate.

"Really!" insisted Reactsslowly. "I've learned my lesson! Anyway, by the time I made it to the last gate, before I got home, I saw the gate was stuck and the waves were getting into the growth pools. I was cold and slow, but it looked so easy. I just had to give the mechanism a little bump. So I did. And, well, the wave came in at just the wrong time, and the gate came down hard just like it is supposed to. Only a few of my appendages were in the way." Reactsslowly wriggled his stumps in demonstration. "So I got confused and forgot to radio in. My bad. My bad. I know. But I remembered to grab my detached appendages to prevent contamination to the growth pool. And I scooted back to the base. Well, just as I was going to the medical bay, I remembered that Human Friend Bob had mentioned a desire to understand Undulate anatomy better. So I figured that I'd just leave my detached appendages where he would find them for study."

Tightensgrimly spread his appendages in bemusement.

"I was hypothermic, in pain, and suffering from main fluid loss," Reactsslowly said defensively. "I mean... otherwise I would have known to put it in the sample refrigerator and not the nutrition refrigerator."

Tightensgrimly wrung his gripping appendages in irritation. *That* was what the younger Undulate thought his biggest failure was?

"Anyway, I leave the detached appendages in the fridge and head down to the medical bay. The medic spends some time telling me what an idiot I am in several different languages… by the way, I am pretty sure he needs to retake human reproductive anatomy because I am pretty sure they can't do the things he implied, and anyway, he hooks me up to an inter-nodal drip to rehydrate." Reactsslowly paused and cringed inward at the next memory. "That was when the sound filled the base. It was high. We heard it in the eight hundred range, but the audio records say that it reached well over a thousand hertz. The hertz range dropped quickly when it turned into words, but that first scream…" Reactsslowly shuddered again. "It tore through my nodes like the coral appendages of some beast of the depths," he said in a low tone. "Bob must have been terribly horrified to have generated such a sound. Poor Human Friend."

Tightensgrimly waited patiently as Reactsslowly slumped in guilt.

"Apparently, when he opened the refrigeration unit, my appendages had fallen on his hand, and before his so-called forebrain could process the most likely scenario, his so-called hindbrain had decided that I was dead and something he calls a zombie."

"What is a zombie?" Tightensgrimly asked in the intervening pause.

"That is something strange," Reactsslowly said. "He was positively ranting about it when he was still inflated on panic, but as soon as he calmed down, he wouldn't tell us anything about these 'undead horrors.'"

"Could this possibly be an example of the previously noted 'superstition concealment reaction'?" Tightensgrimly suggested.

"Possibly," Reactsslowly replied. "But that was one horrified scream for encountering something you don't really believe in."

Humans are Weird – Walking Away

"I have denied the humans' request," snapped Second Mother as she stalked into the Housing Unit Mobile. "I expect all senior research staff to deny it as well. You know they will try to go around my authority with this nonsense Undulate setup."

She tossed her radiation shielding onto her perch and began furiously typing at the data console on the table in front of her.

Gripsstrongly had learned the best ways to interact with the irritable Shatar, and though he did not return to his task, he did not reply to her vague and somewhat insulting statement. Instead he simply extended his appendages as widely as he could in the thin air and observed her. The bright network of her outer membrane gleamed steadily, giving no information about her internals as the humans' did. Her frill laid tight against her neck in what the humans called the 'turtleneck' of irritation. Her angular head tilted this way and that as she aligned her fixed eyes on the screen. Most tellingly, her hands kept coming up to brush at her one good antenna and make swipes at where her other used to be. Finally she noticed his attention and clicked in resignation. She shook out her frill and waved in the direction of the landing field they were constructing.

"The human crew just finished laying the explosives for the demolition of the north rock spire," she began.

"Yes, I received your report," he replied.

"The pale one with the unpronounceable name—" she went on.

"Yökyöpeli," he offered.

"Yes, yes," she said, her frill flicking in irritation. "Him. He came up to me as an emissary for a group of three of them and started asking questions." She paused to let her frill flare to its full extension and then drop back against her neck in a mix of signaling that he thought was meant to express impatience with the ignorance of small children, horror, and utter disbelief. That did not make any sense. "He first asked if I knew the exact time of the detonation," she said. "I answered yes. Then he asked if I knew the exact amount of explosive used. Which I also confirmed. Then he asked if I knew at what angle the sun would be coming in at on a particular long, flat section of ground with a clear line of sight from the horizon to the area where the explosion would be."

"All questions he would have known the answers to himself," Gripsstrongly observed. "Ah, I see your concern. Clearly the human was going to ask for something he knew you would not normally grant and was priming you to be in an agreeing mood."

"Is that what he was doing?" Second Mother asked.

"It is a common human tactic," he assured her.

"Well, then he asked about the placement of the observation cameras," she went on. "Then about their distance and resolution capabilities. Then he asked if I was familiar with the impact resistance stats for human ribcages."

"That is a suspicious question," Gripsstrongly said.

"Then," she snatched up a polishing cloth and brushed it over her eyes to calm herself, "after I made the mistake of admitting that I did not know much about human internal skeletons, he asked to take a 'walking away from the explosion pic.'"

Gripsstrongly lowered his appendages in confusion. "I am not familiar with that term," he said.

"It is exactly what it sounds like," she explained, reaching down to grip the sides of the console. "They wished for one of the cameras to be used to take a picture of them, and I quote, 'slowly and awesomely walking away from the explosion.'"

"On the landform in question they would be within both the zone of force and the zone of harmful particulates!" Gripsstrongly said, beginning to understand her agitation. "I may not know much about human endoskeleton strength, but their auditory and respiration membranes would be horribly damaged! And I am pretty sure they would fracture even those calcium rods they call bones!"

"That was my supposition too," Second Mother said with a grim clack of her mandibles. "When I addressed this matter, he simply replied, 'Don't worry. We heal fast.'"

Humans are Weird – Thanksgiving

"Mostly the date of celebration was determined by when we figured out we weren't all going to die of starvation," the human explained as he hefted the giant carcass into the oven. "So it varies from colony to colony and biome to biome. It's mostly dependent on latitude."

"I see," Quilx'tch observed as he watched from the presumed safety of the top of the cabinet. "But what of the calorie count?"

"What about it?" the human asked as he turned to stirring the mass of congealing animal fat and carbohydrate powder that sat on a heating surface in a ferrous container.

"There are twelve humans here," Quilx'tch pointed out as he took image captures of the cooking process.

"That there are, little buddy," the human confirmed as he bent over a pot of boiling vegetative matter.

"You have prepared enough calories to satisfy three times that many humans for the day of the festival," Quilx'tch observed.

"Nope," the human said, shaking his head, "this is just for one meal. There will probably be leftovers though."

"I had thought that your culture frowned on gluttony," Quilx'tch asked in surprise.

"We do," the human assured.

"But is not this gluttony?" Quilx'tch asked.

"No," the human said slowly as he paused in his constant movement. "I don't think so."

"Why not?" Quilx'tch pressed.

"Huh," the human said as he began moving again. "Good questions."

The door opened, and a second human entered carrying a warm tray of 'rolls.'

"Hey, Carl," the human called. "Why isn't Thanksgiving dinner gluttony?"

"Winter is coming," Carl replied with a cheerful grin.

"Winter?" Quilx'tch asked.

"Didn't they brief you about the axis tilt on this planet?" the first human asked.

"Ah, you refer to the changing of the length of the days," Quilx'tch said with a bob of his head.

"And it is going to get colder," Carl went on. "We mammals need to build up a secondary layer of adipose tissue to draw on when the cold stimulates our metabolisms."

"You deliberately fluctuate your mass with the change of the axis tilt?" Quilx'tch demanded in shock.

"Pretty much," the first human chimed in. "It insulates us pretty good too. Keeps us warm. Now do you want some of the broth off of the veggies?"

Humans are Weird – You'll Make Such Cute Babies

"Do understand... I am not in any way offended, Human Friend Natalie," Sct'sca assured the distressed-looking human. To emphasize the fact, he scampered across the table and patted his paw gently on the soft part of her wrist where her mammalian pulse beat softly. She smiled down at him in relief and shifted to support her chin on her fists.

"Okay," she agreed cheerfully. "I'm glad. It's really embarrassing when your baseline genetic coding gets the better of one like that."

"Ah!" Sct'sca raised one of his primary manipulation appendages to interject. It always made him rather uncomfortable, this interruption of someone else's thought chain. However, the humans had repeatedly assured him that it was not only accepted but necessary for communication with humans. Granted, they weren't as bad as the Winged, but he suspected that that was only because the massively larger mammals just thought slower than the annoying little flighted mammals. "That is my question," he said. "How is what you just did a result of baseline genetic coding?"

The human for once paused for a reasonable time before talking. The fleshy membranes over her eyes pulled far back, showing the gleaming white that surrounded the complex of muscles of her iris. The iris itself dilated and contracted as her brain drew processing power and focus away from her vision centers. Clearly she had to think about her answer.

"Well," she finally began, "we just do that sort of thing. With like... every baby. I'm not a genetic anthropologist, you know, but I think it has to do with making sure the baby is from our tribe? And maybe that it makes us take care of babies who are related to us more?

I remember something about it from secondary school."

She paused and stared down at him expectantly. He processed her words several seconds longer than was strictly required by even the most traditional swarms before replying.

"But there is no baby here for you to analyze... however you do it," he pointed out.

"Ah! Right." She nodded eagerly and cut in with the usual human lack of politeness. "But you are here, and I have seen your wife. So I can sort of extrapolate. Genetic inheritance basically works the same for all us sapients... except the Shatar. And even they still look like their genetic parents. Basically."

Ignoring the odd comments about the Shatar, Sct'sca pondered what she had said. "You claim to be able to extrapolate what our offspring will look like from our appearances," he said slowly, "and that you did this automatically."

"Yup!" she replied with an eager nod.

"Can you give me an example of how you think our offspring will be particularly 'cute'?" he asked.

"Well, you have that curly fur mutation," she said, reaching a finger out to gently stroke the sensory hairs on the dorsal side of his abdomen. "And you are a dark brown. And Triksy has the super thin fur mutation, and she is a very, very light brown. So your babies just might be super soft, fluffy lil balls of caramel when they..." She suddenly stopped talking and squinted down at him with concern.

He quickly realized the source of her discomfort and patted her elbow reassuringly. "Born or hatched are both decent translations," he assured her.

"Born then," she continued. "And of course they will have those big ol' sparkly baby blue eyes and those wobbly lil legs and all the little chirping. Super cute!"

He stared at her in bemused delight for several seconds. How could one not share the clear joy in infants she was displaying? Still…

"All Trisk young share those last traits," he pointed out. "And most sentient infants share several of them. How is that especially cute?"

"But the caramel and the fluffy!" she insisted, waving her hand as if it explained her point.

"And your baseline coding immediately caused you to extrapolate this as the most likely combination of traits for my offspring to inherit?" he asked finally.

"Well, it was the first one my brain suggested," she explained. "They might just be normal baby cute."

Sct'sca pondered this until he realized that it was time for him to head back home to Tcsk'ct. "Well, I will send you holos as soon as they are dry," he said. "You will be able to determine if your extrapolation was correct."

"Thanks, Scitter!" she said with a wide smile. "Can't wait to see them."

After he left he thought to ask if she extrapolated the potential offspring of all of her coworkers.

Humans are Weird – Forgotten

"Who wants to go figure out why the human is wailing in agony?" called out the quartermaster into the officer's meeting.

The reactions of the various Winged ranged from complete disinterest to shocked horror to diving under the nearest display hood in a frantic effort to appear much too busy for such a minor task.

"Is the human in danger?" demanded the newest wing commander.

"Seeing as she is sitting at the meal consumption surface with nothing around her but writing utensils, I doubt it," the quartermaster replied as he began deliberately grooming his wing surfaces.

"She might be in pain!" declared another of the newer flight officers.

"Pull up the display," suggested the quartermaster with a shrug of his wing joints. "It's not likely physical pain."

The new officer did, showing the bases where one human inhabitant was bent around the odd structure called a 'bench' leaning over the 'table,' resting her extended head on her thick, trunk-like limbs. Her swath of blond sensory fur was disorganized and nearly completely covering her face. However, the low agonized roar that she emitted clearly spoke to some distress.

"Is she dangerous in this state?" one of the new officers asked with a nervous chitter. "She clearly hasn't groomed…"

"Don't let that disturb you," the base commander said dismissively as he sipped his morning water. "She almost never grooms more than a handful of clicks before her shift starts. It is a human thing."

"Most humans at my old base groomed first thing," another senior officer interjected. "I think it is just a her thing."

"She's not groomles-mad if that is what is concerning you," the base commander continued. "She has engaged in fully sufficient levels of physical touch with other humans on the base to meet her psychological needs."

"I will go see what troubles her then," the new officer said firmly. "She has clearly frightened all of the others out of the common area."

"You do that," replied the base commander absently.

The younger officer flitted out to perform the task, and a few sensory horns peeped cautiously out of the display hoods to watch on the main display. The Winged officer approached the human exactly to the minimum safe distance for waking a human from sleep and loudly called out a greeting. The human, whose head alone outmassed the Winged by several times, lifted her eyes to him and shoved a mass of sensory hairs out of her line of vision.

"Sir!" she said, stiffening and saluting the officer.

"Are you well, Navigator Jones?" the officer asked.

"Oh, I'm just dandy," the human replied, but she slumped and emitted a loud sigh.

"Pardon my insistence," the officer prompted, "but your body language does not indicate that to be the truth."

The human groaned and let her head fall to the writing surface below her. "I had this really great idea last night," she said.

"Why is that distressing you?" the Winged asked in confusion.

"I forgot to write it down," she explained.

"Well, you can write it down now," the Winged suggested,

flitting a little closer.

"But I've forgotten it!" the human wailed, clenching her fists in a show of aggression though her eyes were aimed at the writing surface in front of her.

Still, the officer darted back out of her striking distance. "Ah, pardon me," he said. "But if you have forgotten the idea, how do you know it was good enough to warrant this much stress over losing it?"

"Oh," the human waved one of her massive hands dismissively, knocking the officer back with the wind, "I do remember it was awesome."

"What aspects were awesome?" the officer asked.

"I don't remember," the human said, glaring at him in exasperation.

The officer flitted around her striking range for a few moments longer while her attention turned back to glaring at the writing surface.

"Well, then," he finally said. "I will leave you to your memory retrieval. In the meantime, could you perhaps refrain from making those noises?"

"What noises?" she asked without looking at him.

"The groans of agony," he replied. "They are disturbing the rest of the crew."

That caught her attention enough for her to look at him blankly for a few moments. The officer clearly shivered and backed away fractionally.

"Sure," she finally muttered before turning back to the paper.

The officer shot out of the room and darted back to the meeting room.

"Good work," the base commander praised him.

"How do they forget the substance of an idea without the associated emotional markers?" the new officer demanded as he landed, shivering on a perch.

"Humans," the base commander said with a shrug. "Moving on to the base energy use."

Humans are Weird – Below the Deeps

"Now tell me all about the incident," Strokessoftly hummed as she ran her gripping appendages over the client who was curled into an impossible tight ball on her algae mat.

A shiver of terror ran over the Undulate's body, and when he spoke, he was clearly strained. "I know the human didn't mean to frighten me," he began.

Strokessoftly hummed in encouragement. The small space of her clinic caught and reverberated the sound. She had spent a great many resources making sure the room was as much like a coral net as any room in a spaceship could be. Half of the interior space was given up to a lattice work of printed coral. Printed with the cells of the most common species on their home world. Beyond that, the walls were all light-giving, creating the illusion of one of the private nooks common back home. It seemed to work because her patient loosened a little.

"But you probably want to know what happened," he said in a resigned tone.

"Tell me at your own pace," she encouraged.

"It was a recreation day," he began. "We were all playing catch on the beach."

"Catch?" she asked when he paused.

"It is a game the humans introduced us to," he said eagerly. "There is a sphere made of semi-dense material."

"How large?" she asked.

As she hoped he would, he loosened his secondary gripping end to demonstrate the size. The tactic worked better than she hoped as this ball was apparently nearly a quarter of their volume.

"So the game in its human form is that they all stand about three body lengths away from each other and propel the ball back and forth between them," he explained. "One human 'throws' and one 'catches.' Think of how we harvest the lipid pods back home... only instead of drifting down into your net you have to catch it with your grippers, and it is coming at you in some variation of a parabolic arc... and at maybe five to ten times the speed."

"That does not sound very feasible for our species," she said, letting some real amusement at his excitement slip through her professional demeanor.

"It's not," he assured her. "They modify it for us. Usually they roll it along the ground. Well, we were all playing catch when Human Friend Steve appeared wearing an insulation suit, one of the old kind that offgas so badly."

"Indeed," Strokessoftly replied.

He had tensed up a bit at the memory, but it seemed to be a disgust reaction to the insulation. "He asked, 'Want to have some fun?' And I said I did. He put on his rebreather, and we went into the water together."

Her patient twitched in amusement.

"Humans are pretty graceful once they are in the water," he observed. "They are amazingly graceful in the air, but when they transition from one to the other, those motile appendages slam into the water like a pair of malfunctioning hydraulics. Anyway, once we got out into the decently deep water, he aligned himself with gravity, and we started swimming."

He paused, and a shudder ran through his body.

"Human Friend Steve kept swimming out," he said. "Out past the marked safety zones and the coral growths. He let his mass pull him deeper and deeper until we reached the underwater cliffs. I was getting colder, and that suit was making me a little dizzy. I lost track of his lights, and when I found him again…" His appendages all wrapped tight to his core. "He had entered a cave and then turned to face me," he murmured. "I could only see his core and his head… and those terrible glowing eyes staring at me out of this dark cavern. Things swarmed in there. I don't think he could see them, but they were like a cloud of unholy minions swarming to his command. I panicked."

"He did not know that we do not thrive well in caves?" she asked.

"I don't think so," he replied. "So I panicked and tried to swim back to shore. I knew it was just Human Friend Steve, but he so looked like some predator of the deep trying to lure me to my doom in the caves, and I couldn't smell him over the suit. I was so confused that I got lost, and they had to send a search team for me. Human Friend Steve was very distressed when I finally made it back to base."

"What was so important that it demanded he explore deep and cold underwater caverns?" Strokessoftly asked.

He relaxed himself with a clear effort and indicated his own confusion. "Nothing," he answered. "He willingly traps himself in cold water under deep layers of weak rock. For fun."

Humans are Weird – Kitteh Rules

"Don't you think the power armor is a bit of overkill?" Tacsk'tch demanded as he wriggled his fourth leg into the suit.

"You were the one who told us the predator had incapacitated a trained human warrior!" Seventy-five Chirps snapped. "I am taking no chances with my soldiers."

"Yes," Tacsk'tch admitted as he pressed the ventral portion of his thorax into the cradle of the suit, "but I think it is more of a cultural thing. Human Dodge was clearly in no distress when I contacted him."

"Enough," barked out Seventy-five Chirps. "Protocol is clear. If a human is incapacitated, all proper precautions are to be taken." He flared his wings wide and aligned the plasma cannons that activated over his shoulders.

Tacsk'tch slumped into the unaccustomed armor and gave up his attempts at argument. He was fairly certain the human in question would not appreciate being disturbed and would appreciate less the disturbance of the apex predator that was the issue at claw. However, a lifetime in administration positions had not really suited Tacsk'tch to argue a point of threat assessment with a wilderness-hardened veteran of a notoriously unreasonable species. (Not as unreasonable as humans but still.)

"Power gear and prepare to move up!" ordered Seventy-five Chirps.

The rest of his flight clicked in response, and a faint hum set the sensory hairs on Tacsk'tch's exomembrane vibrating not unpleasantly. Half the flight darted up into the air to approach the trapped human through the vents while the rest rushed into the corridor. With the advantage of the powered armor, Tacsk'tch had no trouble keeping up along the catwalks. That is until he overcorrected in a turn and smacked into a wall, toppled over the safety rail, fell to the floor dozens of body lengths below, bounced a few times, and skittered to a halt against a box some human had handily left there apparently to stop inexperienced Trisk in power armor.

"I begin to understand why a human's first question on seeing a Trisk is if you can regenerate limbs," Seventy-five Chirps growled over the comm.

"I am alive and uninjured if that is what you are asking," Tacsk'tch informed him curtly. He suspected the fall had jammed half his sensory hairs, but none of his joints were even sprained thanks to the shock absorption.

"Just be thankful your mass ratio is better for that sort of nonsense than a human's," Seventy-five Chirps replied.

Tacsk'tch could hear the relief in his voice however and merely gathered himself up. "I am ready to resume the mission," he said.

"Eh, too late," Seventy-five Chirps informed him. "We are already here. Come along when you can."

"So," Tacsk'tch said. He couldn't quite keep the smugness out of his voice. "My assessment of the situation was correct?"

"If you mean that humans are utterly tailless in thought, then yes," snapped Seventy-five Chirps. "Ranger Dodge is insisting that the predator has him completely incapacitated save for basic reading functions when clearly he could displace it and move away at any time."

Tacsk'tch idly accessed the data feed from the flights as he wriggled around in an attempt to smooth out his sensory hairs. From the looks of things, the Winged were perched in the highest rafters of the room he had found the 'incapacitated' human in. The storage room had a few windows, and the afternoon sun was lighting up the space with a glaring, orange light. Instead of avoiding the glare like a sane sentient, Ranger Dodge had placed himself centrally in the beam, even going to the effort to drag a crate into position to serve as a seat.

Now the Survey Corps Ranger was idly glancing between the datapad he held in one hand and the Winged in the rafters. Meanwhile, his free hand was running soothingly over the predatory fauna they had collected for study several days earlier.

Tacsk'tch smoothed down his hairs as they tried to rise again in jealousy. Sure, you give the humans a nice, fuzzy ally who wants to be petted, and they mutter about primal fears and just give them a little more time to properly file you away in their subconscious. Give them a beast of tooth and fang and claw, and they have it tamed and are petting it in mere days. He slumped and rerouted the unworthy thoughts. It really wasn't the human's fault that he resembled one of their most terrifying predators. Still.

He realized that Seventy-five Chirps had been in conversation with Ranger Dodge for some time and focused on what was being said.

"Sorry," Ranger Dodge said cheerfully. "It is a felinoid; retractable claws, purrs, pointy ears, even toe beans. I don't make the rules."

"I do, in fact, suspect you of making the rules up," Seventy-five Chirps snapped.

"Not this time," Ranger Dodge assured him with a solemn shake of his head. "It is an ancient human cultural law. I cannot move from this location until the kitteh wakes up."

The beast in his lap seemed to give a rumble of assent though the fleshy eye coverings shared by all mammals did not open.

Humans are Weird – Counting Steps

"Greetings, Human Friend Shannon!" Twistunder called out from his perch on top of the stairs. "Might I request assistance?"

The woman glanced around in confusion, and Twistunder feared for a moment that the cold wind blowing in from the rustling grasslands was too powerful for his voice. But eventually her eyes fell on him, and she smiled. She jogged up the stairs and knelt in front of him.

"Hey, Twist," she said, showing all of her gleaming white teeth in a wide grin. "What can I do for you?"

"My mobile assistance unit is malfunctioning," he began to explain. "The cold—"

Human Friend Shannon burst out into laughter and scooped him up in her arms. "No, I'm not you, silly!" she said in a scolding tone. "I'm perfectly fine."

"Humans are not to be viewed as or used as—" Twistunder tried to remind her as he scrambled over her chest to distribute his weight across her shoulders. He was sure the training had been clear about not touching female human pectoral areas, but apparently some factor of 'cuteness' exempted the majority of his species from what was an ironclad rule for humans. Who could understand the social rules of another species? At the moment, Human Friend Shannon was actively mocking the concept that she might be offended if he imposed on her courtesy and used her as a conveyance device. It was odd.

"Never a problem for you, little guy," she said cheerfully. "Now let's get down these horrible bug stairs. Made for a queen, I'm sure, by the size."

"The size does not seem to prevent you from descending them at unsafe velocities," he observed. He expected more laughter, but to his surprise Shannon was rhythmically chanting numbers as they went down. He started as he realized she was counting the number of gradations called steps. She stopped counting when they reached the bottom, and she paused.

"Where to, little guy?" she asked.

"The main commissary please," he prompted.

"Sure thing," she replied. She set out for the commissary at a brisk stride, and Twistunder lightly tapped her shoulder. "Yeah?" she asked.

"How many steps are there?" he asked.

"How many what are what?" she asked in return, reaching up to absently stroke him.

"You were counting the steps in the Shatar-built stair," he observed. "How many of the units you define as 'steps' were there?"

"You heard that?" she asked in surprise.

"I did," he affirmed.

"Good ears, little guy," she said.

"How many steps?" he pressed. It was not really the main question he had, but as she seemed to be avoiding it, he wanted to know the answer.

"I don't know," she said with a shrug.

"You were just counting them," he insisted.

"Yeah," she admitted slowly. "But I always count steps. I don't really remember the number if it is over ten though."

"Why do you perform the observation if you don't intend to

retain the gathered data?" Twistunder asked.

"Good question," Human Friend Shannon replied. "Give me a minute to think on it." As they neared the commissary, she laughed. "I think I figured it out," she said cheerfully. "I think you can blame Sir Arthur Ignatius Conan Doyle KStJ DL."

"Who or what is that?" Twistunder asked.

Human Friend Shannon laughed heartily and wriggled her dorsal manipulation appendages in a request for him to dismount. He did, crawling down her dorsal surface to the ground.

"Counting stairs and other things are just habits I have, Twist," she said cheerfully. "'I see, but I don't observe,' I believe the good detective said. Enjoy your meal."

With that she jogged off, chuckling softly to herself. Twistunder listened to her go and determined to look up this Sir Arthur Ignatius Conan Doyle Night of Justice of the order of Saint John Deputy Lieutenant and determine what he had to do with counting stairs.

Humans are Weird – Bubbles

"So, the humans are giggling again," Thirty-three Trills informed his Wing Commander as he entered the echoing office.

Wing Commander Two Snaps sighed deeply and set down the report he was writing. He stretched out his wings, running the smooth amber surfaces over his sensory horns to clear the fog from his brains. When his back was sufficiently loosened, he released his grip on the perch and fell into the wind.

Thirty-three Trills followed the Wing Commander through a loop without question, and they swept out of the office together. The brisk currents of the corridor woke Two Snaps thoroughly. He didn't bother asking where or who the humans in question were. There was only one crew on the base, and they were currently mobilizing to begin a survey in the eastern quadrant. Given the base schedule, he would find them in the heavy machinery bay.

As he expected, the machine bay was humming with noise and life. A double beat of human footfalls echoed from one of the catwalks. Laughter came in through the open doors. The two Winged fluttered up to the rafters and examined the scene before them. Three vehicles were nearly loaded with scientific gear, and the mechanics were doing final checks on the engines.

"Which humans were giggling?" Two Snaps asked.

"All of them," Thirty-three Trills answered.

"Most of the crew is outside," Two Snaps determined. "We will go observe them."

They dropped from the rafters and flew for the doors, being sure to maintain altitude above the painted safety lines on the walls.

They rounded the door and entered the light just as something exploded over Two Snaps's sensory horns in a wash of suffocating stickiness.

"Knobby fungal growths!" Two Snaps cursed as his horns began to sting and his eyes and nostrils burned. "There're hundreds of them! Take altitude!"

"The wind is blowing them up!" Thirty-three Trills shrieked.

The air around them was filled with head-sized spheres of iridescent something. It reeked. The scent reminded him of humans, but he had never smelled it this strongly.

"Try to make it back to the roof!" Two Snaps ordered. "If we hit the ground, the vehicles—"

"Hey! Here!" a human voice suddenly broke through the pain and confusion. "Here!"

"There!" Two Snaps called out. "A landing!"

A blurry circle of humans had formed, and in their center was a flat surface. The two Winged dove for the point as best they could and fell gratefully into the soft, cool flesh of the hands that caught them.

"Emergency shower!" someone shouted.

In moments, the searing light of the alien sun was replaced by the cool shadow of the bay. There was a loud click, and then he was crushed to the hands by a massive flow of water.

"How long do we hold them under?" someone asked.

"Don't drown them!" another voice cut in.

The flow rate decreased, allowing Two Snaps to thrust his nostrils into the air. He braced himself against the flow and began grooming his horns, noting that Thirty-three Trills followed his example.

"I guess that means they're okay with it?" someone asked.

When the burning on his horns finally stopped, Two Snaps waved for the water to stop and glared up at the human who was holding him.

"Soap!" he spat out.

"Aww! Squeaky... too adorbs!" one human offered.

"Did you say something, sir?" the human holding him asked.

Two Snaps cleared his throat and remembered to lower his voice. "Soap!" he tried again.

"Sure!" the human holding him nodded his head eagerly. "What kind do you want?"

"No!" Two Snaps snarled. "Those things were made of soap!"

"Oh, the bubbles," the humans said more slowly. "Yeah we make them from soap."

"Are you saying," Two Snaps tried to stay calm, he really did, "are you saying that you deliberately filled the airspace of the base with chemical biohazards without informing us?" He was pretty sure the last part of the question had shrieked up into a range inaudible to humans.

"Yes, sir," the human replied in a tone even slower and lower than usual.

"What possible purpose could that serve?" Two Snaps demanded, wondering when his eyesight was going to return.

"We were just celebrating getting out into the field," the human replied. "Bubbles are fun."

Humans are Weird – Wilderness

Blue light from three suns filled a courtyard that was currently cluttered with various survival gear. A single human was busily checking the functionality of a blue water filter as a flight of brilliant red bat-like aliens flitted around him. One particularly bold one landed on his shoulder and reached up a winghook to tug on the human's ear.

"Eh?" the human grunted as he poured the filtered water into the test kit.

"I have a question, Ranger Dodge," the alien stated, lifting his mouth up next to the human's ear.

"No need to shout into my ear, ah…" the human glanced down at the alien on his shoulder and squinted.

"I am Seventy-two Trills," the alien informed him.

"Right, Seventy-two Trills," the human replied. "Ask away." The test kit chimed and flashed a green light, and the human grunted in satisfaction.

"It is the understanding of some of the psychologists in my flight," Seventy-two Trills said as he shifted to match Dodge's movements, "that individual isolation is deeply damaging to a human and should be avoided at all costs."

"You mean solitary confinement?" Ranger Dodge asked as he shoved the filter into his pack. "Yeah, it is considered one of the worst punishments known, and its use is strictly regulated."

The flight of aliens fluttered around him in silence as he continued packing his gear. Finally Seventy-Two Trills spoke up again. "What exactly are you doing now?" he asked.

"Packing for my trip," Ranger Dodge said simply.

"You are going to spend an entire week, entirely isolated from any sentient beings?" Seventy-two Trills pressed.

"That's the plan," Ranger Dodge replied with a grin as he laid his spare underwear on top of his food. The entire flight paused, settling to cling to his shirt and stare up at him, their sensory horns catching the blue light. "Ah, guys?" Ranger Dodge said with a frown. "I need to get going."

"Why," Seventy-two Trills burst out, "are you inflicting this punishment on yourself? Are you in some form of psychological pain from guilt?"

"What?" Ranger Dodge asked with a laugh. "No, no!" He brushed the flight away from his chest, sending them back into the air. "It's not like that at all," he insisted. "I want to do this. It is good for my psychology. I mean it's fun. I enjoy it!"

"What is the difference?" Seventy-two Trills demanded.

"Free will, I guess," Ranger Dodge said with a shrug. "And not being trapped in a small, boring space."

"Free will," Seventy-two Trills muttered as he fluttered around Ranger Dodge's head.

"Look," Ranger Dodge held up the backpack, "if this was something horrible, there wouldn't be a whole industry to support it, right?"

"I question your logic chain," Seventy-two Trills stated.

"Yeah, well, as long as you don't try to stop me," Ranger Dodge said with a grin. "I've been looking forward to seeing those waterfalls for months. Later, little Hellbats."

The flight watched him leave, and Seventy-two Trills heaved a sigh. The position of morale officer was turning out to be more complicated than he had anticipat

Acknowledgments

First to Mom and Dad; who taught me to love reading. To Mr. McCoy; my third grade teacher, who taught me to demand proper grammar. To Don Powers; the most terrifying professor at George Fox University who taught me to expect excellence. To all my little and big English students who have forced me to better understand my own language.

About the Author

BETTY ADAMS LIVES IN A PARTICULARLY DAMP AND REMOTE CORNER OF THE PACIFIC NORTHWEST AND LIKE A HOBBIT ENJOYS VISITORS SO LONG AS SHE KNOWS THEM IN ADVANCE AND KNOWS WHEN THEY ARE COMING. SHE WAS BORN SOMETIME LAST CENTURY AND WILL LIKELY DIE SOMETIME THIS CENTURY. SHE WORKS WINTERS ON A SMALL ORGANIC RESEARCH FARM WHEN NOT WRITING AND SPENDS MOST OF HER TIME HERDING ECCENTRIC GENIUS SCIENTISTS (SHE IS ABSOLUTELY CERTAIN CATS WOULD BE EASIER) WITH THE HELP OF HER GREAT PYRENEES MIX. SUMMERS SHE SPENDS NOMADICALLY WANDERING THE PACIFIC NORTHWEST IN SEARCH OF MATERIAL FOR HER STORIES AND A REGULAR PAYCHECK FOR A BIOLOGY MAJOR (SHE IS REASONABLY CERTAIN THOSE ARE ON THE ENDANGERED SPECIES LIST). SHE HAS SEVERAL WORKS PUBLISHED IN THE NATIONAL PARK INTERNAL DATABASE WHICH MAY OR MAY NOT BE CLASSIFIED DOCUMENTS.

Thanks for reading! Please add a short review on the Barnes & Noble Website and let me know what you thought!

If you are looking for some good heartbreak check out my tragedy.

"Dying Embers: Dragons, Aliens, and Things That go Boomp in the Night"